"I think you'll be safest if you stay at my place, at least for tonight."

"I'm not a stray puppy that you picked up and need to take care of," she informed him.

"No," he agreed calmly. "A stray puppy would undoubtedly be far more grateful."

Orla began to argue with the assumption he had just made. But then, right in the middle, she stopped and laughed. "I guess maybe you're right."

"Does that mean that you're about to continue giving me an argument about coming home with me?" he asked.

Orla nodded. "As long as you keep in mind that I am a martial arts instructor and that I know at least several ways to bring you to your knees without even trying."

His eyes met hers. Sean looked as if he was struggling to keep a grin off his face. He inclined his head. "I consider myself forewarned."

P9-DIF-071

Dear Reader,

You have in your hands what I regard as a minor miracle. Not because it's so good or the fact that this book is on its way to becoming my next hundredth book (granted I have a ways to go before I reach my four hundredth, having already written over three hundred and twenty books.) No, it's a big deal as far as I'm concerned because it exists at all.

When I made plans to write this Colton book, I came down with COVID. Specifically, Long COVID, which blocks out your mind. It was the scariest illness I have ever had the misfortune to come down with. I have been writing stories—books, actually—since I was eleven years old. Suddenly, I was unable to construct an actual sentence. My brain was suddenly so cloudy and, for all intents and purposes, missing in action. I was afraid that I actually couldn't write anymore. It lasted for several weeks but I am happy to say I am back to being me. I wish you all good health and to never come down with this if you haven't already.

I do hope you like this latest effort because you have no idea how wonderful it is to be able to write something when you think you can't anymore.

As always, I want to thank you for reading one of my books and from the bottom of my heart, I wish you someone to love who loves you back.

All the best,

Marie Ferrarella

COLTON'S UNUSUAL SUSPECT

Marie Ferrarella

HARLEQUIN
ROMANTIC
SUSPENSE

Special thanks and acknowledgment are given to Marie Ferrarella for her contribution to The Coltons of New York miniseries.

Recycling programs
for this product may
not exist in your area.

ISBN-13: 978-1-335-73822-6

Colton's Unusual Suspect

For questions and comments about the quality of this book, please contact us at CustomerService@Harlequin.com.

Harlequin Enterprises ULC
22 Adelaide St. West, 41st Floor
Toronto, Ontario M5H 4E3, Canada
www.Harlequin.com

Printed in U.S.A.

USA TODAY bestselling and RITA® Award–winning author **Marie Ferrarella** has written more than three hundred books for Harlequin, some under the name Marie Nicole. Her romances are beloved by fans worldwide. Visit her website, marieferrarella.com.

Books by Marie Ferrarella

Harlequin Romantic Suspense

The Coltons of New York

Colton's Unusual Suspect

Cavanaugh Justice

Cavanaugh Vanguard
Cavanaugh Cowboy
Cavanaugh's Missing Person
Cavanaugh Stakeout
Cavanaugh in Plain Sight
Cavanaugh Justice: The Baby Trail
Cavanaugh Justice: Serial Affair
Cavanaugh Justice: Deadly Chase
Cavanaugh Justice: Up Close and Deadly

Visit the Author Profile page at Harlequin.com for more titles.

To
Jessica
Who Can Still
Make
My Heart
Smile

Prologue

Detective Sean Colton closed his green eyes and rubbed the bridge of his nose, doing his best to make the throbbing headache go away, or at least recede a little. The words on the page before him, words he had written down himself during the course of the investigation, were beginning to crisscross over one another and dance in front of him like some sort of possessed snake charmer.

With a sigh, Sean dragged his hand through his dark brown hair. He had put in later hours on occasion, but he felt as if he really should call it a night or, at the very least, take a break. It felt as if he had been at this for hours.

In reality, he had been at this ever since he had come

home—four hours ago—and for a couple of hours before he had even left the precinct.

He supposed Eileen Reilly, his college fiancée who'd dumped him, was right. He was never going to change. No matter what he promised himself—or the woman he'd asked to marry him, and he had had two of them—somehow or other, the job always managed to come first. That was why the other engagement—to his childhood sweetheart—had fallen through as well.

Both women had dropped him because he tenaciously managed to push on, working on a case, no matter what he promised himself—or his fiancée of the moment—to the contrary.

He had been on the current case he was working on—a case he had been working without a partner, ever since Jacoby had changed departments—for a week now and he felt confident that he had narrowed his list of suspects down to one.

By process of elimination, Sean now believed the person who had to have murdered the beautiful, sweet-faced barmaid who had been the girlfriend of wealthy hedge fund manager Wes Westmore was none other than Westmore himself.

He felt it deep in his gut.

The girlfriend, Lana Brinkley, was found strangled in the Greenpoint, Brooklyn, apartment that they had shared. Neighbors had heard Westmore wailing and lamenting when he had walked into the bedroom and had discovered the badly beaten, battered body. People in the building generally kept to themselves, but when the wailing and lamenting didn't let up, one of the neighbors, or rather several of them, called the police.

Because he was temporarily between cases, this one landed in his lap.

He took an instant dislike to Westmore, he couldn't have even explained why. The man acted as if Lana's death had happened strictly to annoy him. Sean was unmoved by the hedge fund manager, who he felt was just putting on a show for his benefit and strictly to garner sympathy from him.

The people that his heart *really* went out to were the victim's parents. Lana Brinkley was her parents' only child. He gathered that the down-to-earth couple had been so hopeful and so happy when their daughter caught the eye of the wealthy real estate mogul and hedge fund manager and quickly became engaged to him.

According to the neighbors, "who wouldn't dream of gossiping," things went downhill shortly after they moved in with one another.

Raised voices were heard shortly thereafter. One-sided raised voices, which intensified the feeling in his gut that something had definitely been wrong.

Sean had to admit that he was really looking forward to slapping the cuffs on that bastard if he turned out to be guilty. Westmore acted as if it was a real privilege for Sean to occupy the same space as he did.

That was the first thing he had against Westmore, but definitely not the last.

Sean studied the paperwork before him as he chewed on his lower lip. Parents really should be more careful before signing off on their daughters— or their sons, for that matter, he amended. Murder wasn't a one-way street. Just because a person had money didn't automatically make that person blameless—or even a good match. Sadly, he had quite a few stories to back that feeling up, Sean thought.

Placing the photographs he had been studying on the table, he felt they comprised bone-chilling "before" and "after" shots of the barmaid. Westmore had to have been really angry to have done this amount of damage to the young woman, he thought, frowning.

Maybe he was jumping the gun here, but he was really looking forward to bringing this slime-bucket down.

Just then, the phone on his desk rang.

He debated not picking it up, but it just wasn't in him to ignore the call—especially one coming in at night.

"Detective Colton," he answered, raising the landline receiver to his ear. It was an old phone that had belonged to his late father. He just never had the heart to get rid of it after his father passed away.

A female voice on the other end immediately spoke up. "Sean?"

The melodious voice sounded vaguely familiar, although he couldn't put his finger on just why at this moment. It took him a full second to rouse himself. "Yes?"

"Sean, this is Ciara Kelly. Humphrey's wife," she further identified herself. "Humphrey said that if I ever needed anything and he wasn't around, I should call you."

"Yes, of course," the detective readily agreed, immediately focusing as he stood up. Something was wrong, he could tell from the edge in her voice. He spoke to the agitated woman slowly. "What can I do for you?"

Humphrey Kelly was a brilliant psychiatrist who had been their father's best friend and the man who had stepped into their father's shoes when the latter had succumbed to cancer, eighteen years ago. Sean, his younger twin brothers and their baby sister would have wound up being split up and sent into foster care if it hadn't been for the world-famous psychiatrist. Until recently, Humphrey had been a perpetual bachelor.

However, six months ago, Humphrey had surprised all of them by marrying an attractive marine biologist twenty-five years his junior after what seemed like a whirlwind romance.

Sean and his siblings hardly got to know her before vows were exchanged, but it was enough for them that Ciara made Humphrey happy.

There was some hesitancy in her voice as the woman said, "I might be making too much of this, Sean."

"Let me be the judge of that," Sean told the woman evenly.

He really didn't have a relationship with Humphrey's wife, but since the man was important to him and to his siblings, he was attempting to develop one.

As he waited for the woman to answer, he heard her taking in a deep breath before continuing.

"I've been trying to reach Humphrey. He left for the courthouse this morning," she explained. "Anyway, he always, *always* calls me when he gets to his destination. It's just something he does," she quickly explained. "Anyway, he didn't call me and when I tried to call him, I couldn't seem to reach him. To be honest," she continued, a degree of hesitancy in her voice, "I'm afraid that something might have happened to him."

Sean felt slightly uneasy but knew something that might make Ciara feel a little better. "If anything had happened to Uncle Humphrey," he assured her, "I would have known about it."

"You mean like telepathy?" Ciara asked, uncertainty in her voice.

"No, not really," Sean said, trying not to laugh. "Because Uncle Humphrey deals with so many high-profile patients, a long time ago I set up a high-tech distress signal that would have alerted me had there been something wrong. All it would take was a single press on the face of Humphrey's watch or his phone to set off an alarm."

He heard a huge sigh of relief on the other end of

the line. "You have no idea how happy you've just made me."

"Glad to have been of help," he told Ciara.

"But we were supposed to go to a dinner party tonight. It's not like him to just forget about something like that," she added. "He was really looking forward to this one."

This news gave Sean pause. He tried not to let his concern show in his voice. "Let me track Humphrey down," he told Ciara. "Maybe he just got caught up with one of his patients." As soon as he hung up the phone, he called his sister, Eva, now a rookie cop. He wanted to assure himself that his late father's friend had arrived at the courtroom safe and sound. The fact that he never came home tonight was troubling. And the fact that Humphrey's alarm hadn't gone off was only slightly reassuring.

Eva picked up her phone on the second ring. "What's up, big brother?" she asked.

"I need you to check on something for me," he said.

Chapter 1

As usual, Orla Roberts found herself running behind. There were days that it felt as if she was *always* running behind. Not by very much, of course, but just enough that if she slowed down a little bit, she would lose her place and begin to backpedal.

That never happened, though. Orla was grateful that she was good at the various jobs she undertook. And, not only that, she managed to be fast at them as well.

On those very rare times that she lost her place, it certainly didn't take her very long to catch up, she thought with a satisfied smile. Orla took a great deal of pride in what she did.

Had she been like her twin sister, Aimee, she would

have been more than content just to sit back and allow her father, real estate mogul Rockwell Roberts, to pay all her bills, with no thought of ever paying *anything* back. For Aimee, there was no thought of her *ever* paying for anything. It just wasn't done. Not that she was ever appreciative about her father taking care of her finances. She just felt she deserved it. At one point, Orla felt this was how Aimee thought their father showed his love, but now she just wanted nothing to do with her twin. Heaven knew she had tried, but Aimee had betrayed her. So had Orla's boyfriend. She wasn't sure if he had even cared about her. She discovered that he had slept with Aimee because she assumed that he felt there was something exciting about sleeping with both twins.

Well, she thought, they could have each other. As far as she was concerned, they deserved one another and she wanted nothing to do with either one of them. They were certainly made for each other. They were both hateful human beings. She was actually relieved when they were locked up after, much soul searching, she had decided to press charges against them. Aimee and Joe had both been convicted of stalking her.

She should have known her peace of mind wouldn't last. Last night they had managed to escape, each killing a guard in prison. Orla was trying very hard not to panic about this. It wouldn't help the situation. The authorities who called her had reason to believe that Aimee and Joe were headed upstate and that Orla was in no imminent danger. And Orla was someone who could take care of herself.

Orla couldn't have been more different from her twin if she had tried. They were complete polar opposites.

She had been independent practically from the day she'd been born, certainly from the day that she could walk. The path she followed was not one that ordinarily appealed to a young woman who didn't necessarily have to pay her own way. But she actually *liked* paying her own way.

Unlike her twin, Orla thought nothing of working hard at unorthodox careers. The thirty-five-year-old was a trained bodyguard, not to mention the proud owner of a black belt thanks to being a self-defense teacher.

To look at her, a person wouldn't have thought that the tall, slender, green-eyed woman could take care of herself nearly anywhere as well as she could. But there was no question about her capabilities. She carried herself with remarkable confidence and an assurance. It certainly did not come across in any manner of conceit.

Orla also conducted herself with a sense of humor. But if for some reason she felt she wasn't being taken seriously, or even if someone looked at her in the wrong way, the look she shot back at that person would have easily cut them dead in an instant.

Perforce there was a reason for the way she conducted herself. The clients Orla selected were all af-

fluent ones. Choosing people who could well afford to pay her high price gave her the ability to take on pro bono work for women who couldn't afford to pay for help. Women who found themselves stuck in abusive relationships. Women who saw no way out of their situation or were desperately struggling to find a way to free themselves from these relationships—short of suicide, of course, she thought. She couldn't help thinking how desperate someone had to be to even contemplate something of that nature.

Luckily it had never come to that point for her.

Despite the fact that her ex-boyfriend had cheated on her, she had refused to let it break her.

Taking everything into account, she had been born lucky and she knew it. Helping other women who struggled with abusive men was her way of paying it forward.

Not to mention that she was exceedingly good at what she did. Orla also possessed a good eye for detail and the ability to keep those details straight.

Of course, her choice of career, or what she referred to as her career, didn't exactly please her Irish-born mother, Clodagh O'Connor.

But then, not very much pleased her mother, Orla thought ruefully. She had given up thinking it was her mission in life to try to please her mother and get her to come around. Orla marched to her own drummer.

Her parents, like so many other parents she knew of these days, were separated. Her father spent his days selling property at the highest possible market value, steadily building up and amassing the family wealth, and his nights rewarding himself by going out with beautiful women who were half his age, a fact that managed to embarrass her mother no end.

Long ago, Orla decided to follow her own path, adhering to principles that meant absolutely nothing to Aimee. For her part, her twin had never concerned herself with even remotely attempting to curry favor with Orla—or being nice to her. She certainly hadn't cared a fig when it came to doing well by her twin.

Or even pretending to do well by Orla. Heaven knew it definitely hadn't stopped her from having an affair with Orla's boyfriend, Joe Sears, when all three of them were in college together.

As a matter of fact, Orla was fairly confident that her twin thought of Joe as forbidden fruit. Though she wasn't conceited, she knew that Aimee resented her. Orla was convinced that her father thought so as well.

He didn't choose one twin over another; he just observed the situation and she knew that it hurt his heart to see his daughters at odds this way. She had no idea where her twin's jealousy had come from. She had certainly never done anything to lord it over Aimee, or even pretend that she was better than Aimee. But from the time they were little girls, Aimee had always seen their relationship as a competition, one she desperately needed to win. For longer than she dared admit, Orla had longed for a friendship with her twin. She just didn't understand why it couldn't be.

Even her father, who was basically oblivious to things when it came to his family, had noticed Aimee's resentment. It was all but palpable. Orla had been heartbroken over the behavior until she had finally thrown up her hands .

Her concession was not to resent Aimee for her behavior, but to just shut her mind to all of it and take solace in the fact that she was her own person, that she managed to do good and not follow in her twin's path, bleeding her father dry.

"You're going to wind up being late and blemishing your reputation for the first time ever, Orla," she said, addressing the reflection looking back at her in the bathroom mirror. "C'mon, get it together. This isn't like you," she told herself sternly. She didn't like feeling sorry for herself, and she wasn't going to let Aimee's prison escape get the better of her.

She inhaled deeply. She had other reasons to feel out of sorts. After all, she had been working almost nonstop without taking a break lately. She needed to learn how to stop for a breath every now and then.

All work and no play, she silently counseled herself with a resigned smile.

But then, she thought, Aimee was *always* playing, and heaven knew her twin was not a happy camper by any stretch of the imagination. If anything, the exact opposite was true. No, Orla thought, she definitely did not want to be like her twin. Work gave Orla purpose, while Aimee's only purpose seemed to be her rabid desire to get the better of her.

Orla looked at herself in the bathroom mirror. What had gotten into her? She was wasting precious time thinking about her twin and the man who had managed to press her buttons. She had no doubt that the only reason Aimee wanted Joe was because she, Orla, had gone to bed with the man.

Well, if anything had ever existed between herself and Joe Sears, it had definitely died a very quick death.

Although she hated to admit it, she had been rather naive back when she had attended college. For some reason, she was only able to see the good in people.

From there on in, her education had been swift, she thought ruefully. Swift and painful. She never looked back.

She couldn't blame herself because she really had missed the signs at first, signs that pointed toward betrayal. But it really didn't take her all that long to catch on, Orla thought.

She quickly combed her silky light blond hair into place, arranging it so that it didn't fall into her face or wind up at the mercy of the January wind. Neat hair was always the first order of business as far as Orla was concerned.

Orla slowly looked herself over from one side to the other. A pleasing sight could win the judge over very subtly, even if it hadn't been the intention—which of course it was.

Presentation, she caught herself thinking, was everything. It might not have been fair to those who might have presented themselves as less attractive, but that was just the way it was in some cases, Orla caught herself thinking as she hurried out of her apartment.

Still, if what she had to say on her client's behalf was judged on merit alone, she was fairly certain justice would win hands down.

This was not ego. She had thought, long ago, that the idea of having any ego had been stripped from her. What there was, she thought, was only a sense of reality, she comforted herself.

She glanced at her watch. She didn't want to be late, she thought. Midtown traffic in New York didn't leave any room for error.

Her heels hit the concrete, beating out a steady staccato rhythm. With her luck she would wind up with a judge who took it as a personal insult if she unavoidably walked into the courtroom late when absolutely no such affront was meant. She sped up her pace, determined to pick up her client and get her to the court on time.

Chapter 2

Eight hours earlier

Sean's attention was split. Part of it was still focused on locating Lana Brinkley's killer. Try as he might to compartmentalize his mind, he really couldn't get the barmaid's parents out of his thoughts. He had found nothing to convince him that Lana's fiancé wasn't behind her rather untimely demise. As a matter of fact, he was growing more convinced than ever that the jealous, possessive boyfriend was responsible for her death.

However, now he had a more pressing matter: finding Humphrey. After he contacted his sister, Eva, she had reached out to someone who worked at a local precinct located near the courthouse to look into the surveillance cameras there. They wanted to see if they could find any footage that suggested foul play, or anything close to it, involving Humphrey.

A few hours later, Eva had shared the footage with Sean. He could see for himself that the famous psychiatrist had been seen entering the courthouse well before his scheduled time to testify. He was slated to appear as an expert witness in the case of Evan Smith, a man on trial for the shooting death of three men after a bar fight. But Humphrey had never arrived at the trial. And no matter how much he and Eva—and the friend who had sent them the tape he had unearthed—had reviewed the video, neither could find a sign of Humphrey ever leaving the building.

It couldn't have been an oversight, Sean silently argued. It certainly had not been one of those "blink and you'll miss him" moments.

Something had obviously happened to Humphrey. Why hadn't he called Ciara when he arrived at the courthouse? Or at all for that matter? He had to have known that his wife was waiting for his call. And he must have known that he would be missed if he didn't show up at the dinner party that evening.

Sean sighed and dragged his hand through his already rumpled hair, staring at the video for the umpteenth time. "C'mon, Uncle Humphrey, where are you hiding? This is definitely *not* the time to play hide-and-seek," the detective said impatiently to the screen. "You have to know that you're worrying your bride," he said to the person who wasn't there. "If for some reason you didn't have any intentions of calling her, you shouldn't have told her you would."

But even that didn't sound the least bit logical—or like his father's conscientious best friend. Humphrey Kelly was the man who could always be counted on to come through. He never made promises he couldn't keep. He never forgot; it wasn't in his nature. He based his entire practice on living up to his word, he thought with a smile. Eva had discovered that Humphrey had also missed two client meetings that afternoon. This was also completely out of character.

The police world was a dark world at times, he knew that. People didn't live up to their potential. Rather, they lived down to it, doing what seemed inevitable. Men stepped out on their wives, tempted even when they least expected to be. But even if Humphrey had been the type to stray, Sean felt that it was far too early for Uncle Humphrey to be stepping out on his wife. He didn't know the woman personally, but she *seemed* nice enough, he reasoned.

Besides, it had taken him so many years to get serious about a woman and finally commit to one. Humphrey and Ciara had been married for only six months. Humphrey's affections for his new wife were genuine. Yes, it had been rather a whirlwind romance, but that didn't mean it wasn't real. Humphrey didn't play games—he shot straight from the hip. And Sean sincerely doubted that the bloom could have faded from the rose already.

What about Ciara? Could she have been fooling Humphrey? He didn't think she would be devious enough to do so, and he was sure Humphrey was too smart to be taken in that way.

Because he thought in complex possibilities, the thought struck him that perhaps Humphrey's new wife could be lying about the man promising to call her, that he *always* called her when he was supposed to reach somewhere. But a simpler explanation, Sean reasoned, was that it was the sort of thing that a new husband promised a wife, possibly explaining that he couldn't bear to be parted from his bride for even a little while before checking in.

Sean rotated his shoulders. But what if Ciara had been elaborately setting up an alibi for herself, saying he always checked in once he reached somewhere and when he hadn't, she had grown worried?

He was making himself crazy. There had to be a simple explanation for all this, he reasoned.

Okay, then what was this explanation?

Sean glanced at his wristwatch. It was one in the morning, he realized. Just when had that happened?

Sean drew in a deep breath and thought about calling one of his brothers, then decided to call neither Cormac, who was proving himself to be a really gifted private investigator, nor Liam, who was a brilliant ex-con turned NYPD informant. There was nothing to be gained by calling either of the twins at this time.

It was best to hold off until morning. Heaven knew he would be more coherent then, he thought.

If the situation didn't wind up resolved by morning, he and Eva would fill them in then.

And maybe by morning, an answer would wind up rising to the surface, Sean comforted himself. And all of Ciara's fears would wind up being allayed and Humphrey could very well turn up.

Lord knew that the prominent psychiatrist did have his share of enemies. But was there really anyone out there who would want Humphrey dead? Besides, if someone had hurt Humphrey, wouldn't that have been captured on video somewhere on the courthouse cameras?

Eva had uncovered one slightly troubling piece of evidence. But it was hard to imagine someone dragging the psychiatrist off into the utility closet at the end of the hall, Humphrey's last known location, without *anyone* noticing. From all indications, there was a cluster of fingerprints and signs of a struggle within the utility closet, but Humphrey was not a pushover. Sean was willing to bet that the man wouldn't have gone quietly.

Someone would have noticed the man fighting for his life, Sean reasoned, if it had come to that. Those fingerprints most likely belonged to someone else. But they were running tests, just to be sure.

He was getting a really huge headache from all

this, Sean thought as he ran his hand across his forehead. He needed to take a break or else he wouldn't be any good to anyone come morning.

Ever since joining the force, Sean had developed a reputation of cracking more cases than anyone else and faster than all the other detectives. But he didn't get there by pushing himself unreasonably. He did it through steady perseverance, putting one foot in front of the other.

"You're just no fun anymore," he said out loud, reminding himself what his last fiancée had told him when she'd broken up with him and handed his engagement ring back to him. Contrary to what the young woman had initially believed, Sean was not nearly as carefree as he had presented himself.

Small wonder that he didn't have a social life.

Somehow, it was already tomorrow, he thought, looking at the face of the watch he never took off. His watch was specifically waterproof just in case he accidentally got the watch wet or worse, in the event that he made the mistake of taking a shower while wearing it.

It had been known to happen, he thought ruefully, even after all these years.

He was glad he'd contacted his sister and put her on the case. Eva was the one who was closest to Humphrey. The man definitely had a soft spot in his heart for her.

When their father died, Humphrey had been the only one who was able to comfort Eva. Whether it was because he was a psychiatrist, or just because he had an innate ability to talk to troubled souls, Sean didn't know. But their father's friend had spent hours at her side, just talking to her and making her feel better and able to cope with the situation.

This was why she was the right person for the job. Sean knew that she was not going to leave any stone unturned looking for the man.

He needed an outlet, Sean thought. Something to look forward to other than just solving crimes. That used to be enough, he thought, but now he needed something beyond that.

He was going to need all his wits about him if something really had happened to Humphrey. He needed to get a few minutes of rest. Beginning to make his way to his bedroom, Sean only managed to get halfway there. Pausing in his family room, he decided to temporarily sack out on the sofa.

His intention was to simply sit down and just close his eyes for a couple of minutes. He stretched his legs out before him. Then his eyes fluttered shut.

Predictable consequences followed.

The next thing Sean knew, he found himself jerking out of what was a sound, deep sleep. The inside of his mouth felt as if he had fallen asleep chewing on a very large wad of remarkably unappetizing cotton.

Trying to clean his throat, he realized that he needed water, a lot of water.

That was what he got for sitting down and stretching out on the couch, he thought. He knew better.

And then he realized what had woken him up: the alarm from Humphrey's watch.

He leaped up, immediately at full alertness. But as he looked at his watch again, the signal disappeared. Could he have imagined it? Could he have been dreaming?

Sean wasn't about to take any chances. It was time to summon the troops. Aches and pains immediately registered up and down his body. The sofa was definitely not the most comfortable when it came to spending the night, Sean thought. It was the price he paid for surrendering to exhaustion, he thought, stretching and doing his best to snap out of the way he felt.

He actually thought he was made of tougher stuff than this.

Chapter 3

Sean had to admit that he was both relieved and happy that Eva had taken the news about what had possibly happened to Humphrey as well as she had. He'd half expected his sister to freak out. The fact that she hadn't spoke well of her self-control. Her police training had served her well. She had matured. She had come a long way from the little girl who had been beside herself with fear and apprehension after her father died.

Back then, he and his brothers couldn't get her to talk to them. Instead, she'd withdrawn into herself, lapsing into silence. Humphrey was the one who had pulled her out of her tailspin, spending hours with her and bringing Eva back among the living.

Now it was time to pay the man back for his efforts, Sean thought.

Taking on a philosophical bent was not going to rescue Uncle Humphrey. One step at a time, he silently lectured, one step at a time. Maybe by the time they had all gathered together, the threat would actually be behind them.

The first person Sean had called this morning was his brother Cormac, a private investigator. Then he called Cormac's twin, Liam, who had made up his mind that a more peaceful way of life appealed to him. That was why he had turned to the life of an NYPD consultant instead of a con artist.

When Cormac picked up his cell, rather than say hello, what Sean heard was his brother's rather large, loud yawn.

Cormac was known to be an early riser, but only when he had to be. Sean had no idea if calling at this hour qualified.

"Well, that'll certainly get you clients," Sean quipped in response to the noisy yawn.

"Nothing I like better than to begin the day with my big brother talking in my ear," Cormac said crisply. He stifled another yawn. "To what do I owe this pleasant phone call, Sean?"

Daylight was just beginning to creep in through the window. Sean was busy making coffee. He assumed that his siblings would want coffee first thing in the morning and this was their "first thing."

Measuring out the coffee, he poured in the grounds.

It instantly began to make noise. "Are you busy, Cor?" Sean asked.

"That all depends on what you mean by busy," his brother answered. "I was just in the middle of this really great dream."

Sean could tell that his brother was grinning. He wasn't in the mood for a light-hearted exchange. Not when it concerned Humphrey. "Table it," Sean ordered his brother curtly.

"This sounds serious," Cormac responded carefully.

"Oh, it is." That is, unless things have changed since in the last few hours.

He could almost see Cormac crossing his arms before him. "Okay, talk."

"Let me preface this by saying that this very well could be nothing," Sean began.

"I've never known you to sound this serious about 'nothing,'" Cormac said. "Tell me what's going on."

"Well, unless things have changed recently Humphrey seems to have gone missing."

"Come again? What do you mean he's gone missing?" he wanted to know.

Sean took a breath, beginning at the beginning. "According to his wife, whenever he puts in a public appearance at a courthouse as an expert witness or to give his deposition about how reliable a witness actually is, Humphrey always calls her when he gets there to let her know that he has reached his destination. As you know, Humphrey has his share of enemies," he told his brother.

"Well, this time around, he did *not* call her. Not when he got there and certainly not when he told her he was leaving. That doesn't sound like him," Sean said. "So I put Eva on the case. We were able to access the video feed from surveillance cameras at the courthouse. Nothing," he declared in frustration.

"How soon do you want me there?" Cormac asked.

"As soon as you can," Sean told him.

He could hear Cormac's bed creaking. "On my way. I just need to get dressed."

"By all means," Sean said wryly. "Get dressed."

He called Liam next. It wasn't anything that he had ever deliberately planned, calling one sibling over another, it was just because that was the way things turned out.

The phone continued to ring on the other end of the line. Was Liam out somewhere?

Sean was just about to hang up when Liam finally answered.

"This is Liam," the deep voice announced, even though Sean had caller ID on his cell. "Can I help you?"

"Well, it's about time, Liam. I was about to give up on you," Sean said. "You don't usually sleep through your alarm—I take it that your alarm did ring this morning?"

"Tell me, did you call to find out if my alarm is working or was there some other reason for you calling me so early?"

"I take it that you haven't heard?" Sean asked.

"I'm not even sure I've heard this conversation

yet," Liam said. "All I know is that you don't usually call at this ungodly hour—unless you want something, of course. *Do* you want me to put in a little legwork for you?"

When Sean didn't respond to Liam's teasing, he must have realized there was a problem.

"Okay, I apologize. This is obviously serious. You just threw me, because you don't usually call this early with something serious. What's up?" he wanted to know. "Is it a two-alarm fire, big brother, or a five-alarm one?" he asked.

"It's not a joke, Liam," Sean replied.

"Obviously. You know, you really need to get more sleep than you're getting, big brother."

He could all but hear the frown aimed in his direction. "When I want to be coddled, I'll let you know. Right now, I just need you to get over here." He paused. "Ciara called me last night."

Ciara was not Liam's favorite person and Sean knew it. For Humphrey's sake he had always made an effort, refraining from saying anything. "And?"

"It seems that Humphrey always calls her when he's supposed to arrive somewhere important. You know, court or a big meeting."

"And?" Liam prodded again.

"And he didn't call."

Liam tried to put the pieces together. "You mean he never got there?" Liam questioned.

"No, according to the courtroom video tapes, Uncle Humphrey *got* there," Sean answered.

"So what's the problem?" Liam asked pointedly.

"Well, he never called his blushing bride to tell her that he did," Sean said.

Liam didn't see the problem—but then again, he wasn't as close to Humphrey and Ciara as Sean was. "So? Maybe they had an argument and he didn't feel like calling her. We don't know what the argument was about and maybe Uncle Humphrey didn't feel like making up with his blushing bride just yet. We don't know what their marriage is like and we only have her word for it that he calls her whenever he's due somewhere. Maybe this is a knock-down, drag-out fight."

Sean looked at the phone receiver in surprise. "Oh come on, when has Humphrey *ever* behaved like us mere mortals?" he asked his brother. "Mere mortals with feet of clay?" he further described.

"If he was a selfish man, I'd say never, but Humphrey has never behaved like a selfish, mere mortal," Liam confessed. "To be honest, when I was a kid, I used to check if there was daylight coming in beneath his feet. There were times when I didn't quite think he was real. At least, he struck me as being too good to be true more than once."

"Yeah, me too. To be honest, I almost felt guilty, liking him as much as I did. Dad seemed more real, Humphrey didn't. He always seemed to know just what to say, what to do," Sean admitted. "Part of me couldn't understand why the man never got married. The other part was jealous that he found someone when he finally did."

"No doubt about it," Liam agreed. "Humphrey Kelly is a very complicated man."

"Well, the first thing we need to make sure of is that everything is all right," Sean pointed out. "But I have a sinking suspicion it isn't."

"Wait a second," Liam said, calling his attention to one important fact, "does Eva know Humphrey didn't call?"

"Oh, she knows," Sean assured his younger brother.

"Oh, Lord," he groaned. "How is she handling this? I can remember when Dad died, she was hermetically sealed to Humphrey. To the man's credit, he put up with it."

"We have to find him," Sean told Liam.

"You don't have to convince me. I'll be there as soon as I can," he promised.

"I'll hold you to that," Sean said.

"I totally expected that you would," Liam replied.

He began to hang up when he heard the doorbell ring. The family was gathering together, he thought.

Time to get to work.

Chapter 4

"Is that smile for us, Sean, or is someone else coming to this little impromptu tea party of yours?" Eva asked as she wiggled in through the open doorway of her older brother's apartment. She had thought that by this point, Sean would have moved into a larger apartment but since he spent most of his time at work, she supposed this small space would do just fine.

"Us?" Sean asked as he began to close the front door after letting Eva in. "The only person I see is you."

"That's because I tend to capture the spotlight whenever I walk into the room," Eva said. But for all her joking, Sean could see the tension in her face.

"She said modestly," Liam added, pushing the

front door open just before Sean had a chance to close it in his face. "Hello, little sister. I didn't expect to see you here first thing in the morning."

Eva spun around to face him.

"Don't call me that, Liam," she admonished, referring to his habit of calling her his "little sister," "unless you want me to call Cormac your better half."

"Well, everyone else knows that's already true," Cormac said, walking into the foyer and completing the sibling reunion in Sean's apartment.

"Hail, hail, looks like the gang's all here and we can finally get this meeting started." Sean walked over to the front door and flipped the lock closed. "Everyone help yourself to some coffee," he prompted, gesturing toward the kitchen.

"That's it, just coffee?" Liam asked, sounding disappointed as he looked around the room.

"I had no idea I had to tempt you people to come over. I would have thought that solving a problem involving Humphrey would have been enticement enough," Sean said. "Besides, we don't get together that often these days."

"Which is why you're the innocent brother," Cormac said, pretending to pat Sean's cheek. Sean caught his younger brother's wrist, pushing his hand away. "Lucky for the rest of us," he announced, "I am fully aware of our big brother's lack of imagination." The jest rang hollow, despite his best efforts, with the sadness at Humphrey's disappearance lingering in the air.

Cormac placed the large bakery box he had picked up on his way over on the small kitchen counter, tucking it next to the coffee machine. The coffee machine made a noise as if it were greeting the pastries.

"Oh look, Cormac even taught the box of pastries to say hi," Eva pointed out in amusement.

"I have my hidden talents," Cormac quipped, the corners of his mouth curving.

"All right, are you finished?" Sean wanted to know. He knew his siblings were trying to add some levity to a very difficult situation, but enough was enough.

"I was born ready," Eva said. "Not that any of you big lugs ever noticed."

Now that he had their attention, Sean backed off just a little. He didn't want to seem as if he was making too much of the situation in case Humphrey had turned up and just hadn't called for some reason. But Eva was already in the loop, and she was of the same mind as he. Humphrey was in some kind of trouble.

"As I told all of you when I called, Humphrey's wife called me late last night," Sean began.

"Does she usually call you?" Liam asked.

"How about never?" Sean responded.

"She was nervous. According to her, whenever Humphrey goes to offer his testimony in court, since he's doing something out of the ordinary, he calls her when he gets there."

Liam frowned. "That doesn't sound like something Humphrey would do."

"Neither does getting married, and yet he did," Eva pointed out. She shrugged. "People change."

It was Liam who pinned Sean down to get to the heart of the matter. "So, is there anything new to add?"

"Well, there is one thing," Sean told them, keeping an eye on Eva to see how she would receive the news. "I think Humphrey's alarm buzzed this morning."

Eva's eyes snapped his way. "I was going to tell you," Sean said. "But it woke me out of a deep sleep, and by the time I looked at the phone, the distress signal had stopped. I tried to trace it, but I couldn't."

"And you haven't heard from Ciara this morning?" Cormac asked.

Sean topped off his coffee. Unlike his brothers and sister, who took their coffee with varying degrees of cream and sugar, Sean took his coffee totally pitch black, in some cases just slightly lighter looking than mud.

"Nope," Sean answered. "She didn't call. I'm afraid that might make things worse for her. If Humphrey had turned up, Ciara definitely would have reached out to us. As it is, she must be worried sick. I will follow up with her soon, though."

Eva frowned. She said what everyone was thinking. "Come on, guys, this is Uncle Humphrey, our second father. Hell, our *only* father for the last eighteen years. None of us wants to entertain the idea that something happened to him. He's supposed to be invincible. As long as he is all right, *we* are all right," she pointed out. "I can understand Sean not wanting to confront the possibility. I don't condone it, but I can understand it."

"You don't really believe that, do you?" Liam asked.

She frowned. "No, but it's something to cling to. First order of business," she said, dusting off her fingers on the napkin that sat at her place setting, "is for you to call Mrs. Kelly—" referring to the woman formally "—and find out if he ever got in touch with her. Or hopefully, actually came home."

She was right, Sean thought. He had never had this sort of problem tiptoeing around things before. He had always faced whatever problems he encountered head-on, whether it was getting a killer to confess, or proving someone innocent of a crime, even though that person looked as if they were about to be convicted by everyone else.

What was wrong with him now? Sean silently demanded.

Added to that, he had never had a problem getting back to the family of a victim before. He had always made a point of it. Why was he having such a problem now?

He knew why. He just didn't want to put Humphrey's mortality into words. Who could blame him? A man he cared for like a father, who had stepped up to care for him and his siblings when he really had no obligation to do any of that, might very well have his life at stake if he and his siblings didn't react properly or quickly enough.

It was a hell of a thing to face.

Putting down his coffee mug, Sean picked up his phone and began to dial.

Eva never took her eyes off her oldest brother. "So, are you calling Ciara Kelly?" she asked him.

He nodded.

In his own mind, he had to admit that he did harbor a degree of doubt about the woman but those doubts were outweighed by the guilt he instantly felt when Ciara immediately picked up in the middle of the first ring.

Sean could hear Ciara breathlessly asking, "Humphrey, is that you?" He knew she must have caller ID, but the desperation in her voice—she clearly wanted her husband safe and sound—made him sad.

The fact that he had suspected Humphrey's wife of making this entire thing up made Sean feel instantly guilty. He silently apologized to the woman, although he refrained from saying the words out loud.

"No, Ciara," he told her. "It's Sean Colton." He saw his sister indicating that he put the call on speakerphone so that the rest of them could hear what Humphrey's wife had to say.

He promptly did.

"Did you find him?" Ciara asked eagerly. "Is he all right? He *is* all right, isn't he?" she asked when Sean didn't answer immediately. "Isn't he?" she repeated. There was a hitch in her throat.

The next moment, it sounded to all of them as if Humphrey's wife was crying.

"So you still haven't heard anything from him?" Ciara responded negatively.

Sean sighed. "That's just it," he added. It killed him to have to admit this. "I don't know. The good news is that there is no sign of violence at the court-house—we aren't sure if the signs of struggle in the courthouse utility closet are due to Humphrey fight-ing with someone—but we're going to check that all out for ourselves once we get over there. I just wanted to find out if Humphrey texted you or emailed you before we go to the courthouse to see for ourselves."

"We?" Ciara questioned.

"My siblings and I," he explained.

"No," she answered unhappily. "There's been no email, no phone messages, no communication of any sort. I just want you to understand that this isn't nor-mal for Humphrey," Ciara stressed. "Ever since we began going together, whenever Humphrey would go somewhere out of the ordinary, at least for him, he would *always* get in contact with me." A concerned edge entered her voice. "Something's happened to him, Sean. I just know it."

"Let's not get ahead of ourselves yet, Ciara," Sean said.

"What else am I supposed to think?" she wanted to know, her voice cracking. They could all hear her fighting back a fresh set of tears in her voice.

"You can think positive thoughts until it's proven otherwise," Sean told the desperate-sounding woman.

"And if it's not?"

"Well, thinking positive thoughts will give you the strength to continue, and who knows? We might all turn out to be right."

He heard the woman sighing audibly. "Do you really think so?"

"I have to," Sean told her. He wasn't speaking as a police detective. He was speaking as Humphrey's friend. "Besides, I've known Humphrey a lot longer than you have. The man has been through a lot and he has always turned up unharmed—without even a scratch to mar his good looks.

"Someone once planted a bomb in his building," Sean recalled, citing a specific situation. "And Humphrey came out of that without so much as a single mark on him."

"There's always the first time," Ciara said, very concerned.

Sean placed a hand over his phone. "What do you say we go see her first, just for a few minutes before we hit the courthouse?"

The frown on Eva's face suggested they would be wasting precious time they didn't have to waste, but Cormac and Liam indicated that they were all for offering Humphrey's wife a measure of comfort in person.

Eva raised her shoulders in an exaggerated shrug,

conveying to Sean that he was in charge and that she would go along with anything he felt was necessary.

"Does that mean you're okay with it?" Sean asked.

"I'm okay with it," Eva answered, although her tone suggested otherwise.

Good enough for me, Sean mouthed to the others. He would have never expected his sister to go along with his decision so easily.

One less battle to fight, he mused. A zillion more to go.

"Listen, Ciara," Sean said aloud, "if it's all right with you, we'd like to come over before we go to the courthouse to look the place over. You know, touch base, get a list of places Humphrey might possibly have gone at the courthouse."

"Fine," Humphrey's wife immediately agreed. "I'd be more than happy to see you. Just find my husband for me. I haven't slept a wink all night."

"Then we'll be right over," Sean said. "Cormac is just the person you need. He's guaranteed to put you right to sleep. All he needs to do is say a handful of words," he told Ciara. "And I promise that you'll be sleeping in no time flat."

She laughed sadly at his words. "I promise you I won't be able to sleep until I know Humphrey is okay," she responded. "How soon can you get here?"

"As fast as the traffic and the speed limit will allow."

"Say twenty minutes?" Ciara asked.

"Fifteen is more like it," Sean answered, terminating the call. "You guys ready to go?" he asked.

"Lead the way, Detective," Liam said to his older brother.

Chapter 5

Orla lost no time in swinging by her client's temporary home—the safe house where she had stashed Rachel Smith so that her stalker wouldn't be able to find her before the judge could issue a temporary restraining order. Not that the restraining order alone would make the man keep his distance from the young woman, but it would certainly help.

This way, she would have something to show law enforcement if it came down to that. Something with teeth, Orla thought.

She chose to walk to her destination instead of grabbing a cab. Half the time, Orla had discovered, walking in midtown traffic proved to be a great deal faster than driving in it. Besides, walking was excellent exercise and as far as she was concerned, she never seemed to get enough of that.

Moving quickly, she managed to reach the hotel door just a tad earlier than she had initially predicted. Orla gently knocked on her client's door, but didn't get a chance to identify herself before she heard the young woman hesitantly ask, "Orla?"

Orla sighed. She had developed an elaborate signal for her client to use between them so that she didn't get caught up in any trap that Teddy, Rachel's stalker, could use to get into her living quarters.

Worried about her, Orla had already moved the woman three times to make sure she remained safe. Orla had even paid for a bodyguard friend of hers—using her own money—in order to keep Rachel safe. After all, she couldn't be everywhere at once, and she felt that it was money well spent.

Orla's father was a real estate mogul who had absolute buckets of money and he was more than generous with it. Money had never meant that much to Orla. What did mean something to her was doing a decent job and, of course, keeping her client safe. Orla never wanted another living human being to wind up going through what she had suffered at Joe's hands.

What she had once mistaken for affection turned out to be almost rabid possessiveness. She wasn't able to make a single move without his coming down hard on her. Moreover, Joe had made her feel that it was all her fault.

When she finally realized what was happening,

she set Joe straight and subsequently broke up with him. At that point, Orla learned that Joe was sleeping with her twin and had been for a while.

If it was in her power to do so, she would have just eliminated all the Joes of the world by gathering them up and sticking them all on an island.

"Yes, Rachel, it's me," Orla responded. "This is where you ask who 'me' is."

"But I already know who you are, Orla," the young woman said innocently, still talking through the door.

Orla suppressed a sigh. Rachel was as sweet a person as anyone she could have ever wished to encounter. Sweeter, most likely, Orla thought. But as far as her client being bright, well, that was another story entirely.

"Do you want me to pretend not to know?" Rachel asked her, her eyes widening as she opened the front door to admit Orla. Orla could tell that she was being perfectly serious.

Even though she had no intention of remaining with her for any length of time, Orla locked the door behind her. With any luck, she hoped she could get Rachel to pick up that habit, although she didn't hold out that much hope.

"What I want is for you to go on living, Rachel. What I don't want is to have to rip that slime bucket's heart out in order to make him pay for threatening you and for trying to intimidate you. The law might not understand why I decided to extract his heart through his nostrils," Orla explained. "Not unless the judge ruling on the case ever knew anyone who had ever been stalked. That sort of memory is extremely difficult to get over."

"Did you?" Rachel asked, genuinely curious. "Ever know anyone who was stalked?" she asked, completing the rest of her question. Her expression was the soul of innocence.

Orla frowned slightly to herself. Ordinarily, she did not get personal with her clients, other than telling them that she understood how they felt. Sharing her feelings was not part of the deal. However, in this one instance, she really felt that making a clean breast of her previous situation would help move this along for both of them.

As for Orla, at least her ordeal all those years ago would have served a purpose, she thought.

Rachel smiled at her "protector" gratefully after Orla finished relating her own experience. "Can I offer you something to drink?" the young woman asked, moving into the tiny kitchenette. "Maybe a little breakfast?"

The table was set for one. If she were to make a guess, Orla would have speculated that the young woman she was protecting had already eaten and that this was set for her.

"I've had breakfast," Rachel went on to tell her. "But it wouldn't take me any time at all to throw something together for you." And then she flushed. "Not really throw together for you," she amended, embarrassed at her choice of words. "But you know what I mean."

She knew exactly what the young woman meant.

And, more to the point, exactly why Rachel's stalker had picked Rachel as his subject. The timid woman was the perfect person to order around. From what she had pieced together, Rachel had tried very hard to do everything her boyfriend wanted. But no matter what, it never seemed to be enough. It was a no-win situation.

The poor girl was wasting her life because no matter what she tried, her stalker would never be satisfied. Chances were, she would wind up dying trying to please the man. Orla had seen enough of these terrible cases. She wasn't going to allow this case to be among the ones that ended badly.

When Orla had walked in, she noticed that Rachel had had the television on, undoubtedly for company. She had done that herself on more than one occasion, Orla recalled. But right now, she didn't need to be distracted.

Orla was about to ask Rachel if she would mind turning off the television when a story she was definitely *not* expecting came on.

A very classy-looking reporter was dressed impeccably in an outfit that came with what had to be a rather high price tag.

"This just in. Aimee Roberts, the daughter of real estate mogul Rockwell Roberts, and her boyfriend, Joe Sears, both convicted of stalking two years ago, escaped from a New York prison last night. The police are conducting a manhunt for the duo, who are believed to be armed and dangerous. Authorities do not know where they might have gone, but speculation is that the couple, once romantically linked, will try to get as far away from Manhattan as they can."

Stunned, Orla turned toward Rachel to find the young woman staring at her. "Are you all right, Ms. Roberts? You've suddenly gone as white as a snowstorm," Rachel exclaimed. Her eyes widened. "Is there something wrong?"

"Yes," Orla whispered, still staring at the television screen. Her entire life had just taken a turn for the worse. She thought they'd be escaping and putting miles between her and themselves, not turning up possibly close by.

This was bad, Orla thought. Very, very bad. The words all but drummed in her head. She thought she'd have a little more time before the story went public. How could she keep a low profile and protect her client when the whole world was going to be seeking her out?

Her twin and her twin's ex-boyfriend had been sent to prison for their crimes against her and her father. When they were finally apprehended and sent away, Orla had breathed a huge sigh of relief, believing that her father, whose only sin was not showering Aimee with an endless collection of gifts just for existing, was finally safe.

But now her hateful twin as well as Aimee's sick lover had made good their escape. She just *knew* that the first person they were coming after was her father. She would bet anything on that. The second person they were coming after, she thought, had to be her. Maybe they were heading upstate for now, but Orla felt it was just a matter of time before they came back to New York.

She could not remember a day when her twin hadn't had it in for her. Aimee's hatred had no rhyme or reason to it, but it existed nonetheless. And now that Joe had thrown his lot in with hers, she would bet that her former boyfriend was out to get her as well.

Distressed, Orla attempted to come up with a course of action to undertake in order to rectify the situation. Yes, she had to protect her client, she thought, glancing at Rachel. However, she also needed to protect her father.

She was certain that the man didn't believe he was in any danger from Aimee, but Orla didn't have that luxury. The more she thought about it, the more convinced she became that Aimee and Joe weren't heading upstate, no matter what the authorities believed.

"There's been a slight change in plans, Rachel," Orla said, turning toward the young woman.

Rachel looked at her uncertainly. "What sort of a change?" she wanted to know, then quickly added, "You're the boss."

"I'm going to ask James to take you to court to see the judge ruling on your case," she told Rachel.

"James?" Rachel questioned, confused.

"Yes, you remember. James Holman," Orla prompted. "I had James stepping in as your bodyguard during those instances when I had other obligations to see to," she reminded Rachel, attempting to reassure her. The last thing she wanted was for

Rachel to become nervous and upset. "He's the one you said was so nice you couldn't picture him doing anything that even had him raising his voice."

Rachel's face lit up. "I remember him," she told Orla. And then she glanced at her watch. "But can he get here in time?" she asked, worried. "I don't want to be late getting to court."

Oh, if there were only more people around like this woman, Orla thought, the world would be a much nicer place.

"You won't be," she promised. "James will have you there on time. I have never known him to be late."

Rachel looked rather doubtful, but she offered no argument about that stance. Instead, like the docile, even-tempered person she was, Rachel went along with her protector's position. "Whatever you say," she told Orla.

Gratitude flooded over her. She had to be the best client she had ever worked with. "I'm cutting your fee in half," she told Rachel.

Rachel looked at Orla in surprise. "Really?" she cried. "You don't have to do that," the young woman protested.

Now Orla was more convinced than ever. Once she was certain that her father was out of danger, she was going to find a way to make this all up to the young woman. It was just that, right now, she needed to make sure that her father was protected. That meant, like it or not, her father needed to be placed in protective custody.

She was sure that her big, tall, strapping, movie star–handsome father would just love hearing that. But it was necessary, even if her father didn't like it.

Nothing harder to take care of than an unwilling client, she thought—unless it was a client who was also a parent.

"Oh yes, I do," Orla assured the young woman. "And I promise that I won't forget this kindness."

She called James. She found that she didn't need to explain the situation to him. As it turned out, he had been listening to his TV over breakfast and had heard the story about Aimee and Joe's sudden and irritatingly successful prison escape.

"I need you to take Rachel to court today. The judge is about to issue a restraining order against the creep who's been stalking her," she explained, filling the man in on what was happening. "I need to get over to my father's place."

"I can be over there in a few minutes," he promised.

"Knew I could count on you. Thanks, James, I owe you—big-time," she told him just before she hung up.

Chapter 6

Driving two vehicles, the Colton siblings arrived at Humphrey's apartment. It was a place they had all grown up intimately familiar with. It seemed painfully empty now without Humphrey's presence.

As per their agreement, the Coltons were briefly meeting with his wife, to reassure the woman that they were doing everything in their power to find the psychiatrist. And to ask if she had anything that might help them figure out where Humphrey is.

Sean was about to take the lead. He felt that if he helmed the meeting, his siblings could focus on ignoring the awkwardness they felt in the woman's company.

But upon entering the apartment, rather than even saying hello, Eva got right to the heart of the matter.

"Have you heard anything from Uncle Humphrey yet?" she asked. And just like that, the siblings forgot about the awkwardness they experienced in Ciara's company and became totally focused on finding answers to their questions.

One look at Ciara's face told the siblings that she hadn't heard any more now than she had when she'd initially called Sean.

"Can I offer you anything?" the woman asked, closing the door behind the Coltons.

It was a vaguely worded offer because if any of them had requested something, Ciara didn't look as if she even knew where to find it. She looked like she was just sleepwalking through her existence.

"Is there anything we can do for you?" Sean wanted to know.

Ciara didn't hesitate. "Find Humphrey for me."

"That's what we intend to do," Sean promised, squeezing her hand. "Is there anywhere that Humphrey likes to hang out when he goes to the courthouse? Does he have any clients who have been upset with him lately?" he asked. It occurred to him that they knew very little about a man who had been so important in their lives. He and his siblings had tried to come up with a suspect list on the way over to Ciara's apartment, but they'd come up blank. Except for one possibility...

Ciara shrugged her slender shoulders. "Not that

I know of. I don't ask him questions about his day," she confessed. "You four know him better than I do. He's pretty closemouthed when it comes to his patients and his work. He keeps his client files locked up in his office and he has never shared any of his confidential information."

She attempted to sit down, but really couldn't. Instead, she kept flittering around, moving from one place to another like a bird unable to find a perch for itself.

Ciara looked at Sean, her eyes pleading with him for reassurance. "Do you think he's all right?" she asked nervously. "If anything happened to him, we would have heard about it, wouldn't we?" she asked.

"Uncle Humphrey's a very famous psychiatrist. Besides, if anything happened to him, I'm sure we would have heard about it through the police grapevine," Sean told her. "The rest of my motley crew is going to go to the courthouse to check it out."

"But not you?" Ciara questioned.

"I've got something I want to follow up on," Sean told her.

Ciara wrapped her hand around his, anchoring Sean in place as if what he said to her was the most important thing in the world.

"And you'll call me the very moment you find out anything at all?"

Sean nodded. "The very moment," he promised Humphrey's wife.

Taking him at his word, Ciara walked all four of

the Coltons to the front door. Sean turned to look at her before he and his siblings left. "Maybe you would be better off if you went to work, Ciara. Try to get your mind off what's happening," he suggested.

But Ciara shook her head. "I can't think, can't focus," she admitted. "I wouldn't be doing anyone any good at work."

They walked out of the apartment in silence. No one said a single word until they were well out of hearing range.

Eva broke the silence first. "For the first time since we've found out about Ciara, I actually feel sorry for her," Eva admitted.

"Yeah, me too," Liam agreed.

"All right," Eva said, turning toward Sean. "Just what is your plan? While the rest of us scour all the nooks and crannies at the courthouse looking for clues, what are you going to be doing, big brother?"

Sean paused next to his vehicle. "Humphrey once told me that if anything ever happened to him, I should go and question Rockwell Roberts about it."

"Rockwell Roberts?" Liam asked, rolling the name over in his mouth. "You mean the real estate big shot?"

"One and the same," Sean answered.

"Why didn't you ever mention that to the rest of us?" Cormac asked.

"Hey, I don't tell you everything," Sean said. "Besides, until now, there was no need to share that little tidbit."

Eva frowned. "I would have rather been prepared than not," she told Sean.

"I'll keep that in mind for next time."

"Hey, wait a minute," Liam cried. "I think I heard something on the news this morning mentioning Rockwell Roberts. The guy's got a daughter who just escaped from prison. The news said that she and her boyfriend, who was also sent away for a crime, killed two prison guards and made their getaway last night."

"Obviously Roberts's daughter does not believe in that old nursery rhyme about 'sugar and spice and everything nice,'" Eva commented with a dour expression on her face.

"This is beginning to sound more and more complicated," Cormac commented.

"Maybe we should have dug a little deeper into Humphrey's practice," Liam suggested, wondering if the prison break had anything to do with Humphrey being missing.

"We investigated as much as we could in this limited time frame. If he doesn't turn up soon, we can investigate the situation further. I doubt Humphrey would appreciate us digging into his life if we can avoid it," was Cormac's opinion on the matter.

Eva turned on her brother. "How could you say that? This is Humphrey we're talking about. He wasn't just Dad's best friend, he was there for all of us when Dad died. No matter what he's into, we owe him more than we can ever repay," she insisted.

Cormac frowned. "I hate to say it, but *little sister* here has a point."

"You bet I do," Eva insisted. "And if you don't stop calling me that, you are going to have major regrets," Eva warned her brother. Her eyes swept over all three of them.

"I owe you, James. Big-time," Orla told her friend the moment she let the man she had called into the rented room.

"You would do the same thing for me," the bodyguard told her.

"True, but that doesn't take away from the fact that I'm really grateful to you for coming out so fast."

The six-foot-three bodyguard nodded at Rachel, then looked at Orla as he walked in. "You really think that your father's actually in any danger from your sister?"

"When it comes to my sister, I *never* know what to think—but I always expect the worst—and I am never disappointed," Orla told him. "Aimee thinks that the world—meaning my father—owes her a living. I have no idea why she thinks that way, but I know for a fact that she does."

"You know, I never asked you, but what's it feel like, having someone walking around with your face?"

Orla never hesitated. "Awful, because people think she's me."

He laughed. "That resemblance vanishes within a

minute. That woman is *nothing* like you," James said. "Two seconds in your presence and a person would immediately know that."

Orla smiled, appreciating his assessment. "You're very sweet," she told him. "And I meant what I said. I owe you for this."

"Just let me know how this goes." Turning toward Rachel, he gave her an encouraging smile, and asked, "Are you ready?"

Rachel let out a shaky breath and nodded her head. "I'm ready," she answered.

"Good luck," Orla told her client. "Just listen to James and do what he says. You can't go wrong."

Rachel's head bobbed up and down. "I know. Good luck with your father," she said, flashing Orla an encouraging smile.

Orla was out the door in moments, her heart racing as she mentally crossed her fingers. She was really hoping that she wasn't being too laid-back, too lax about the situation.

At this point in her life, although she liked keeping a positive attitude about things, she was afraid that she wasn't viewing what her twin was capable of seriously enough.

Or maybe she was guilty of making too much of the situation after all. If Aimee had a brain in her head—and she knew that her twin did—she would be trying to make good her escape. She wouldn't be still here, looking to get her revenge against their dad. The police seemed to think she and Joe were long gone, headed north.

Maybe she was being too logical, she thought as she hailed a taxi and traveled to her father's large, sprawling apartment in Gramercy Park. For as long as she could remember, Aimee had always been driven by her desire for revenge, not to mention money.

Her heart hammering in her throat, Orla arrived at her father's apartment in what felt like record time.

Edgar, the doorman, nodded his head, smiling broadly the moment their eyes met in the lobby.

"How nice to see you again this morning, Ms. Roberts," Edgar said by way of a greeting.

Again.

The single word beat like an unnerving drum in her head, stealing her breath. "Again?" she finally repeated, her stomach twisting.

The doorman's smile widened as he nodded. "You didn't think I saw you, did you?" he asked, obviously pleased with himself. "But I did. I saw you tiptoeing into the foyer earlier this morning, heading toward the elevator. It's none of my business, but when I didn't see you leaving, I just assumed that you were still in your dad's apartment, Ms. Roberts."

Aimee was here.

Horrified, she could feel her apprehension throbbing not only in her throat, but in her chest as well. Orla felt as if she was trapped in some sort of horrible dream.

The first thing she thought of was asking the doorman to summon the security guard, but the security guard wasn't trained to deal with a potential killer, which was the way she viewed her twin. She had no doubt that Aimee wasn't here merely to yell at her father; she was here to make him pay for turning his back on her and allowing her and her lover to be sent to prison.

How could she have been so stupid, Orla upbraided herself, and brought that awful person, Joe, into her life?

Granted it was twelve years ago when she was in college, but thirteen years was *not* a lifetime ago. She was brighter than that.

She *should* have been brighter than that, Orla thought. For a second, she was at a loss as to what to do and where to turn. But the next moment, she reminded herself that she had always looked inward for strength.

Now was no time to change her approach.

But there was a time to rely on herself and a time to turn to the police, and this was definitely a time for the latter.

The doorman looked at her with concern. "Is there something wrong, Ms. Roberts?" he asked her. "Do you need me to do something?"

Orla did her best not to sound as agitated as she felt. "I just need you to stay behind your desk and do what you've always done, Edgar," she told the doorman.

"That's all?" he asked, sounding almost disappointed.

Orla already had her phone out and was focused on dialing 9-1-1.

"That's all," she assured him.

Sean Colton chose that moment to walk into the foyer, looking around and attempting to orient himself. He had been to a great many locations and buildings on his way up from NYPD officer to homicide detective. But he had never been inside of this particular one.

The distressed-looking woman in the lobby caught his eye. She looked like the type of woman he would have expected to find living in a place like this, classy but distant.

Well, unless she was a witness, he didn't have time for her.

Seeing the doorman in the foyer, he approached the man. "Excuse me, I'm looking for Rockwell Roberts," he said. "Could you tell me if he's in? Or, if he isn't, where I might be able to find him?"

"Why are you looking for Rockwell Roberts?" Orla wanted to know. She was sure her suspicion showed on her face as she regarded the man standing in the foyer.

Was this one of the people who had helped her sister and that creep of a boyfriend of hers escape from prison?

Or maybe even worse, she couldn't help wondering. If nothing else, life experience and dealing with Aimee had taught her to be extremely cautious about who she trusted.

Quite honestly, there were very few people she could trust.

Practically no one.

It was a horrible way to live, she knew, but at least she *was* still alive.

Orla looked at the man questioning Edgar. Granted, he was extremely good-looking, but that most likely was actually contributing to his sense of entitlement.

Her eyes narrowed. "Just why are you looking for Rockwell Roberts?" she asked again.

Chapter 7

"I could ask you the same question," Sean said to Orla. "Why are you so interested in Rockwell Roberts?"

As the doorman came up, looking ready to send Sean on his way, Sean flashed his badge at him. "This is official," he told the man.

The doorman relaxed and smiled. "Looks like you're in luck. This is Mr. Rockwell's daughter,"

Orla frowned more to herself than at the stranger. She would have preferred to save the introduction until she found out just why this man was looking for her father. Though she had nothing to base it on, she couldn't shake the feeling that there was something wrong. But Edgar had managed to take that element of surprise away from her.

"I was told to look for him if anything ever happened to my friend Humphrey Kelly," the stranger explained.

Orla shook her head, unfamiliar with the name. "I'm afraid I don't—"

She was about to claim her ignorance but again, the doorman spoke up. "Ms. Roberts, that's the famous psychiatrist who's always being called to testify as an expert witness in court. The guy's practice is pretty packed, although I didn't know that he and your father were friends. Although I suppose it stands to reason. They tend to move in the same circles," he told Orla with authority.

The doorman seemed to make everyone's comings and goings his business. "You never cease to surprise me, Edgar."

He smiled, taking that as a compliment. It was obvious that he was pleased with himself. "Glad to be of service, Ms. Roberts. It looks like your dad is a very popular man today."

The words immediately alerted Orla. Was that just a harmless observation, or was there more to it?

"What do you mean by that?" As a rule, although her father did a great deal of business, he never did it on his home turf. Home was for kicking back and recharging his batteries. On occasion, home was for being able to talk to her when Aimee had gotten to be too much for him to put up with. That stopped when Aimee and Joe had gotten arrested and sent to prison.

But now that the duo had escaped, Orla no longer knew what to expect.

Most likely the worst, she thought, her pulse speeding up again. Turning toward the doorman, she said, "Edgar, I need you to call 9-1-1."

"There's no need for you to call the police, Edgar," Sean told the man authoritatively. "I am a police detective," he reminded the doorman, touching his badge again.

Orla looked at the man next to her skeptically. "Could I see some proof?" she requested.

"Gladly," he responded, taking out his wallet and opening it for her benefit, showing her his I.D. "I'm Sean Colton. Could I ask why you need a detective?"

This was going to sound really strange to the man. But it didn't make the situation any less true, she thought, a wave of helplessness washing over her.

"Because of what I'm afraid I am going to find upstairs in my father's apartment," she told the detective.

"And that is?" Sean prodded.

Orla took a deep breath. "My twin sister and her boyfriend were sent to prison for stalking me. They escaped from prison last night."

Edgar's mouth dropped open as he stared at Orla. He instantly realized the mistake he'd made. "Oh, Miss Roberts, I'm so sorry about this," he profoundly apologized. "I didn't realize—"

Orla waved away the man's apology. "Don't worry about it. A lot of people used to make that mistake. My twin sister always used it to her advantage," she told the doorman. "As a matter of fact, she would count on it." Frowning, Orla looked upward, at a loss as to what to expect and how to handle it.

"You really think she's capable of doing something violent?" Sean asked her.

"Oh, much more than capable," Orla told him with conviction. She hurried over to the elevator. Waiting for it to arrive, she glanced toward the detective. "By the way, I'm Orla Roberts, Aimee's twin sister."

"Under the circumstances, I can't really say that it's a pleasure to meet you, but we'll work on that."

He pressed for the elevator. "Maybe it's not as bad as we think," he told her.

"This is my sister," Orla responded. "I know *exactly* what she is capable of." She drew in an apprehensive breath as her imagination took off. "We might very well be walking into a bloodbath."

"Like I said, I hope you turn out to be wrong." The elevator doors opened but he put his hand up, stopping her. "You stay here. I'll let you know what I find when I come back down."

Orla stared at him. He had to be kidding, she thought. "When you what?"

"When I come back down," the detective repeated. "You wait in the lobby," Sean said, loudly and clearly as if he were talking to a small child.

"I will certainly do no such thing," Orla informed

him tersely. "If anyone is going to go upstairs to see just what havoc Aimee has caused in her wake, it's going to be me. You're welcome to come along if you want, but I *need* to see what Aimee did, otherwise my imagination is going to create a terrible scenario."

The detective paused for a beat as the elevator arrived.

"Let's go," he urged, gesturing for her to begin walking ahead of him.

When they reached Roberts's floor, they got out and Sean asked her, "Do you have a key to your dad's apartment?"

This was New York City. He knew that in some cases, people were rather strange when it came to admitting to having keys to living quarters that weren't their own.

"Yes," Orla all but bit off impatiently, "I have a key to my father's apartment."

Orla made her way over to a secondary area that wasn't immediately evident at first.

Sean's brow furrowed as he took in the area. "Is this something new?" he asked her.

"Different," Orla told him. "My father had it installed for his private use," she explained. "He had it put in to allow him a private escape from the paparazzi and the people who felt that their particular position in life entitled them to get exclusive, private access to one of the city's wealthiest men. He had people picking his brain as well as attempting to get his money."

"Do reporters get that bad?" He sounded surprised.

Orla rolled her eyes. For a police detective, he seemed almost naive, she thought.

"Worse," she informed him. "This way," Orla urged as she gestured for him to follow her.

Access to her father's living quarters was available through yet another separate doorway. Her heart hammering in fearful anticipation, Orla walked into the apartment directly in front of Sean.

"The lights are on," Sean commented, looking around. "I guess your father's home."

But she shook her head. "That doesn't mean anything. The lights are always on. It's a habit of his," she explained. "Even when my father's not home, he leaves the lights on."

For a second, a fond smile slipped over her lips. "When I was growing up, the lights were always on," she told Sean. "At the time, I thought that everyone always kept their lights on like that. It was only when I was older that I discovered this was a very specific habit that belonged only to my father."

Turning, she crossed another threshold.

Suddenly, the detective grabbed Orla's arm and pulled her toward him, turning her face away from whatever it was that had alerted him. He pulled her over so quickly, she almost stumbled as she swallowed a gasp.

"Don't look," he warned her sternly.

Alarmed by the detective's tone, Orla was immediately on her guard.

"What's the matter?" she demanded, attempting to pull away as she frantically scanned the entire area.

The next second, Orla had her answer.

Her father was on the floor, a massive pool of blood having oozed beneath him. The blood was already beginning to dry. Her father had been savagely beaten and shot.

"Oh, Daddy!" Orla cried. She pressed her fisted hand against her mouth, trying desperately to stifle the sound that was attempting to escape her lips.

For a moment, engulfed in sadness, she let the tears fall freely down her cheeks. Sean held her against him, not saying a word. What was there to say, really?

For just a split second, Orla clung to the detective.

And then she straightened, growing rigid in his arms, returning to the tough-as-nails bodyguard that she was.

"I'm all right," she told him stiffly, pulling back.

"No, you're not. That's your father on the floor, and unless you're completely heartless, you are definitely reacting to the sight. And that's all right," he insisted, "because you're allowed to feel something. You're allowed to grieve, for heaven's sake."

As if to protect herself, she asked, "You think so? Then you don't—didn't," she corrected, "know my father very well. He was a difficult man to deal with." Sadness echoed in her voice. "And you could never risk turning your back on him."

Sean stared at her, as if amazed by the words coming out of her mouth. "Do you really feel that way?" he asked her, appearing stunned.

She took in a deep breath. "Answer something for me."

"If I can," Sean responded.

"Why are you here?"

Orla's question caught Sean off guard. But as he rolled it over in his head, he realized that the victim's daughter did have a point. He'd told her he was here because his father's friend had said that if anything ever happened to him, Sean should immediately check on his whereabouts by questioning the mogul about Humphrey.

"I already told you why," Sean reminded Orla.

"Exactly," she agreed. "As much as I hate giving any credence to that sort of theory, we both know it might be a possibility," she told him. "My father could have been involved in your friend's disappearance—or could have known who was." She waved him onto his phone to make the necessary call. "Go, call in those CSI people who are so good at finding clues," she urged. "Maybe they can point you in the right direction and find some sort of indication that my sister isn't responsible for any of this—although I sincerely have doubts about her innocence."

Actually, he did too, but he was not about to say so out loud until he had proof, one way or another.

Getting off the elevator, Sean went to place his call to the CSI team, keeping an eye on the victim's daughter. He was not completely convinced that this was now all behind them, or that Roberts's other daughter was finished carrying out her little vendetta against her sister, her now late father and possibly any other family member that she might have had it in for.

This, whatever "this" turned out to be, was not over with by a long shot.

The doorman seemed to materialize out of nowhere and immediately overheard the detective talking to someone official about what had happened. The doorman was instantly alert.

"This is the most excitement this building has seen in years," the doorman told. The next moment, Edgar's face became exceedingly contrite looking. "I am very sorry about what happened to your father, Ms. Roberts," he told her.

"Yes, so am I," she said in a quiet voice.

"You know, it's amazing how alike you and your sister look. If you hadn't told me that you had a twin sister, I would have never believed that it was possible for two people to look that much alike," he confessed.

"Aimee's not all that happy about it, either. That's why she's been trying to get rid of me all these years," she said bluntly. "For some unknown reason, she was always convinced that my father always favored me over her."

"Did he?" Edgar asked innocently.

Sean, now finished with his call, was curious to know the answer to this too. He knew that sibling dynamics were always complicated. But if he knew more about their relationship, it might offer him a clue as to what might happen next. "No, he did not," Orla told the doorman. "What he did seem to favor about me…" she continued, her eyes filling with tears. She paused to banish them. "What he did favor about me," she repeated, clearing her throat, "was that I never asked him for anything. That I always worked for a living and was determined to provide for myself when I didn't have to, while my twin," she ended matter-of-factly, "was forever pumping our father for money."

Chapter 8

Sean debated clearing his throat so the man's daughter would realize he was there, then decided that since this was a homicide and he had practically been the first on the scene, he was going to ask to work the case. And if that was granted, he was going to need as much information as he could gather together on the matter.

Orla must have seen the doorman looking over her head. She turned around and frowned. "You know, a more polite man would have cleared his throat, signaling that I should stop talking," she informed Sean.

He inclined his head. The woman was right—sort of. "I suppose, but a polite man wouldn't be as consumed with curiosity about you as I am," he pointed out.

Orla's eyes met his.

"Just why are you here, Detective?" she asked him. "Were you attempting to run down an empty lead, or did you just happen to get lucky?"

"I don't consider walking in on a homicide as 'getting lucky.' *Stopping* a homicide," he emphasized, "*that's* getting lucky. The thing I have against the nature of my job is that I'm hardly ever in time to prevent tragedies from unfolding. The few times that I am, *that's* what I count as being fortunate."

Orla's eyes swept over the man thoughtfully. "You know, you are a rather complicated man, Detective Sean Colton."

"So I've been told," Sean responded.

"I'll bet," she replied.

Sean looked at her, wondering if he was reading her correctly. "Ms. Roberts, you're not by any chance hitting on me, are you?" There was no conceit in his question. He couldn't deny that he was attracted to her—and if he wasn't mistaken, it went both ways.

That could turn out to be a problem, he couldn't help thinking.

Her eyes widened. "Oh God, no," Orla denied so quickly and with such vigor, Sean wound up laughing.

"Well, there goes any ego I might have been nurturing," he told her, tongue in cheek.

Orla looked stunned, as if she had no idea how to respond to his comment. "I wasn't looking at you in any sort of new way," she finally told him.

"All right," he said, picking up the thread of the

conversation, "Just exactly what sort of light were you looking at me in?" he asked, wanting nothing more than to untangle this word riddle he found himself in.

"A truthful one," she said. She did what she could to explain her way of thinking. "You don't strike me as someone who fabricates things in order to grab center stage, or to make himself look important."

Sean looked at her, but she wasn't attempting to flirt with him, he realized. Strange though it seemed, the woman was just telling him the way she perceived the situation.

Sean couldn't help thinking that the exceptionally attractive woman gave him the impression of being no-nonsense. She didn't insult his intelligence by trying to flatter him or invent stories that made her appear in a complimentary light. She just told it the way it was.

From what he had learned in passing, the woman's twin liked to play games—and always, *always* win them.

Playing that sort of game each and every time had to be utterly exhausting, Sean couldn't help thinking. He knew it certainly would have exhausted him.

Studying the property tycoon's daughter, Sean came to his own conclusions. If nothing else, Orla Roberts struck him as being a very honest, sensible woman. Honesty came with a very high ranking in his book.

"I'm guessing that you're nothing like your sister. Are you?" he asked.

For a moment, Orla's eyes flashed.

"No," Orla bit off. "Were you told that I was?" she challenged.

"I wasn't told anything. I'm just going by my own compilation of facts. Going with my own gut instincts." He had seen the news reports. "What threw me was the fact that you look just like her, so it's rather hard to absorb the fact that you are completely different from the woman who's walking around with your face," he told her.

"Is that your actual opinion," she asked the detective, "or is that what you think I want to hear?"

"No matter what you might think, Ms. Roberts, I don't lie just because it might be convenient to do so. I was raised to only tell the truth, no matter what," Sean said with unwavering conviction.

Surprisingly, Orla smiled. "You know, you sound so sincere, I could almost believe you."

Sean laughed softly under his breath. "You really should," he advised.

The wary look in her eyes began to dissipate as she carefully considered his words. After a moment, Orla put out her hand to his.

"Clean slate?" she asked.

Sean's smile mirrored hers. "Clean slate," he echoed, nodding his head. And then he asked, "Is there anything that would have led you to believe that your twin was going to kill your father? After all, she and her collaborator just made good their escape a few hours ago. They could have gone anywhere, but you lost no time in getting here as soon as the news about their escape was made public. Were you that sure your sister would try to kill your father?" he asked.

"I was 99.9 percent sure," Orla informed him. And then she let out a long, shaky breath. When she spoke, her voice quivered and almost broke. "And, heaven help me, I was right. With all my heart, I really wish I wasn't, but I was." Tears rose in her eyes again. "Heaven help me, but I was," she repeated under her breath.

Touched by what he saw, Sean didn't say a single word. Instead, he just drew Roberts's daughter into his arms, holding her and silently comforting her as best he could.

At first, determined to be strong, Orla attempted to push Sean away but she just couldn't seem to create any distance between them.

She didn't want him to think she was some sort of a wilting flower.

"I don't want you getting the wrong idea. I'm not the type of person who just completely falls apart at the first sign of any kind of adversity."

"You just found your father dead on the floor of his apartment. You would have had to have been a robot not to be affected," he insisted. "And no matter how hard you try to project that image, you are *not* a robot." Taking her face in his hands, he looked down into her eyes. "There is no way that you're going to convince me that you are."

Another very shaky breath escaped her. "Just what I need," she told him, a sad smile lifting her lips. "A bossy male."

He drew back to look at her for a long moment. "Right now, maybe yes," he acknowledged with a nod.

Because he was treating her with kindness, Orla found that his words just had her falling apart more quickly. Giving in to the tears that were building within her, she put her head against his shoulder and let herself cry for a couple of moments, sobbing her pain.

A few moments later, Orla did her best to regulate her breathing and not break down again.

"I'm all right now," she said rather stiffly.

"Give yourself a few more moments. There are no extra points for catching your breath faster than you *think* you're supposed to," Sean told her.

"Do the people who work for you accuse you of being bossy?" she asked him. There was a hint of an amused smile in her voice.

"All the time," he admitted. "And so do my siblings."

"Siblings," she repeated. She hadn't thought of having something in common with the detective, but obviously, she did. "How many do you have?"

"Three. It's been them and me for the last eighteen years. I'm the oldest, in case you're wondering."

"Eighteen years. That would have made you a kid at the time."

"Depends on your definition of a kid," he said. "But if it helps clarify things for you, I was eighteen at the time." He paused for a moment, then continued. "We have something else in common, except that in my case, it's slightly removed."

She looked at him as if he had lapsed into another language. "English, Detective, English."

"There are twins in my immediate family as well," he said.

She looked at him in surprise. "You have a twin brother?"

"No," he answered.

"Then why..."

"But the twin in the family has a twin brother," he went on to tell her. "It's a smaller world than you might think."

"And are those twin brothers of yours the kind that you just turn your back on?" she asked.

"Actually, no. We depend on each other. We have ever since my father died of cancer."

"What about your mother?" she asked.

"She passed away a few years before then," he told her.

"Oh, I'm so sorry to hear that," she said. He had suddenly become a person to her, not just a police detective.

"When my father died," Sean continued, "we became orphans. Except for Humphrey Kelly. He was the reason my siblings and I weren't shipped to a group home or separated and sent off to foster homes. We owe him. So when he disappeared a couple of days ago and his wife called me, I felt that we owed the man more than we could ever repay. As I mentioned earlier, Humphrey once told me that if anything ever happened to him, I should go and try to locate your father and talk to him."

"My father?" she murmured, confused. "Why?"

Sean shrugged. "I don't know. That part was left up in the air," he admitted to her. "Do you have any thoughts on the matter?"

Orla shook her head. "I'm coming up empty," she said. "The only thing I know about your benefactor is what everyone knows. He's a famous psychiatrist who gets called into court to act as an expert witness at least several times a year. I heard that he was supposed to be in court a couple of days ago, but as to how that went, I have no idea."

"It didn't," Sean said. "That's why I came here, looking for your father. Because while Humphrey was caught on camera showing up at the courthouse itself, there is no record of him either testifying in any of the courts that were in session that day or even talking to anyone official inside the courthouse."

"Well, he couldn't have just disappeared into thin air," Orla protested.

"No, he couldn't have," the detective agreed. "The dilemma is where do we start to look. And," he quietly reminded her, "this is my problem, not yours, Ms. Roberts."

She shifted, giving him a warning look. "Don't you start putting up barriers between us now," Orla told him. "It would just wind up being a huge waste of time on your part."

Chapter 9

That was the moment that Julio Flores, one of the CSI team, chose to stick his head into the room. "Detective Colton, I need to have a word with you if you don't mind," the man requested.

Immediately alert, Sean turned to face the man. "Is there something wrong?" he wanted to know.

"You mean other than having one of the richest men in the state murdered in his own home?" Flores asked with a touch of sarcasm. "No, I just wanted to check a point of procedure with you."

Sean's eyes shifted toward Orla. She looked so vulnerable to him, he didn't want to just walk out on her. "Do you mind?" he asked her. "I'll be right back."

Orla nodded. "Take your time. I need to catch my breath and clear my head, anyway."

Sean really didn't feel right about leaving the woman alone at a time like this. But he knew he really couldn't say anything like that because it might sound as if he was insulting her.

This was a very delicate position she found herself in. All he could do was place one foot in front of the other and proceed with caution. "I won't be gone long," he promised.

She waved away his statement. "Don't worry about it," she told him. "I'll be fine. You're not responsible for me."

He had a different opinion about that. In a way, he felt responsible for everyone he came in contact with. He knew saying so out loud would just drag them into an argument, so for now, he counteracted her assumption with a suggestion. "Why don't you go down to talk to the doorman and ask if he saw anyone else stopping by to talk to your father, or if he directed someone toward your father's private elevator?"

He was creating "busywork" for her, Orla couldn't help thinking, but there was also a possibility that it might even help. At any rate, she decided, it wouldn't hurt.

"Sure," she agreed. "I can do that."

"I'll come looking for you as soon as this is taken care of," he promised.

She nodded. Rather than take the elevator—they always made her feel trapped when she took them by herself—she opted to take the stairs back to the ground floor. Besides, taking the stairs on her own always made her feel more in control of the situation.

But the doorman, Edgar, was nowhere to be seen. "Okay, Edgar, where are you?" she murmured, looking around the foyer. She hadn't interacted with the man a great deal, but he'd never struck her as the type who took advantage of any sort of commotion to slack off or sneak away.

When she did finally locate him, Edgar was talking to several of the tenants, undoubtedly answering questions about why there was a CSI vehicle parked near the entrance.

This, she thought, was undoubtedly going to take some time. She'd go crazy just loitering in the lobby waiting for the detective to return. She felt as if the walls were closing in on her.

She decided to go back to her original plan and get a little air. She pushed the revolving door, exiting the building. The cold air hit her immediately, assaulting her cheeks. Despite the fact that it was the middle of the day, it *was* cold.

She definitely shivered. She pulled up her collar and wrapped her coat around her more securely as she walked out onto the street. It was packed.

Had this been any other time, she would have enjoyed walking around, clearing her head and just enjoying the hustle and bustle of humanity that milled around her.

But not today. Despite the fact that, at bottom, she was a New Yorker, it felt as if there was a very heavy weight on her chest.

Part of her hadn't come to terms with what had just happened, that for no reason other than her twin's baseless, mindless jealousy, her father was permanently gone out of her life.

Orla could feel fresh tears filling her eyes and sliding down her cheeks. She didn't need any clues to convince her that this was Aimee's doing.

She knew.

"She's not going to get away with this, Dad," she whispered into the shadows, then swore, "I won't let her."

Orla and her father had never really been all that close. Maybe that was even partially her fault, Orla thought, because she had drawn into herself— although Rockwell was an unethical liar. Maybe the fact that she'd been so independent had created some of that distance. And now she would never have the chance to change things.

Orla could feel her jaw tightening, as she clenched her fists at her side.

"You're going to be sorry for this, Aimee, sorry you killed our father. Sorry that you were ever born," she quietly promised with feeling.

A movement caught her eye.

Actually two movements caught her eye simultaneously. Sean had just pushed through the building's revolving door. Spotting her, the police detective waved at Orla, indicating that she should make her way back across the street and into the building.

At the very same time that Orla saw Sean, she heard the distant screech of tires.

The tires sounded as if they were drawing closer.

The driver was approaching in a brand-new large black vehicle. Caught by surprise, Orla let loose with a bloodcurdling scream. Before she could react, Sean sprinted and threw himself at her, managing to pull her out of the way by a hair's breadth. The car only narrowly missed them.

Orla hit the sidewalk, the cry throbbing in her throat as the detective cradled her in his arms.

The screeching sound filled the very air and for a second, she didn't even realize that the noise was coming from her.

Orla was clutching at Sean's shoulders as she made her way up to her feet. For his part, Sean pulled her to him and away from the scene just in case the vehicle's driver changed his or her mind and returned to make good on the near collision.

"Are you all right?" he asked, doing a quick inventory of every inch of her.

Her legs were shaking as she tried to stand. "I am, thanks to you," Orla said as the significance of the whole situation finally began to sink in.

Several people who'd seen this almost fatal meeting of flesh and metal came out to gather around the woman who had come very close to being a fatality and the man who had saved her from that fate.

Questions were being fired at both of them from several directions as onlookers took out their cell phones, filming like crazy in hopes of capturing a decent video of the event that had just happened.

"C'mon, let's get you inside," Sean urged. He raised his hand, placing it between Orla and the people engaged in snapping what transpired.

"Step aside, people," he ordered. "Give her some space. The woman needs space."

"I'm okay," Orla told him, doing what she could to reassure him despite the fact that inside, she was shaking.

Sean placed his arm around her shoulders and was gently guiding her back into the lobby.

"No," he told her, curbing his temper. "You are not. You are definitely *not* okay. Don't you realize what could have happened to you? You told me that you were going to go wait out in the lobby, not take a stroll out in the middle of traffic," he reminded her. "You could have been killed."

Orla had never reacted well to being lectured. "I wasn't taking a stroll out in the middle of traffic, I was crossing the street, going to the other side."

"In New York, that can amount to one and the same thing," he informed her angrily. "Someone killed your father. For all you know, they could be after you too."

If that had been her sister behind the wheel, then

this had just escalated up another notch—if not more. Her stomach felt as if it was tightened.

Orla realized she was shaking, which both embarrassed and angered her—but it didn't negate the fact that he was right.

She looked at the detective. "I think you're right," she told Sean quietly. "I'm probably going to need my own protective detail around me."

They had entered the lobby and taken the elevator, then he carefully escorted her back to her father's apartment.

At this point more than over half of the area had been worked over as a crime scene and cleared. That was the area that they wound up keeping to.

"This is highly unusual," the man said to Sean. "We don't usually let in anyone onto the premise piecemeal, not until it has all been processed and cleared."

Sean nodded. "Well, this is rather an unusual set of circumstances," he told the other man. "Don't worry, I'll take full responsibility for the situation."

Flores nodded thoughtfully. "Well, considering that you're Captain Reeves's fair-haired boy, I suppose it's all right. Just try not to make a habit of it," he cautioned.

Sean glanced over toward Orla, who, despite everything, was barely holding it all together. "I doubt very much if Ms. Roberts has any intention of trying to make a habit out of this sort of thing." With that, he made his way over toward her and directed her away from the others. "I'm going to be taking you home with me when I finish working this area."

"No, you're not," she responded without hesitation.

"From what I gathered, you don't have anyone that you're close to," he reminded her, "So yes, I am. I'm not taking a chance that whoever did this to your father might have the same thing in mind for you. You practically just got run over. Who's to say he or she is going to just give up at one try? They just might be the stubborn type."

"So now you're in the business of paranoia?" Orla asked him. He suspected she was trying to mask her vulnerability.

"I'm in the business of keeping people alive so they can see another sunrise," he informed her tersely. "The paranoia's just an added perk."

Her eyes met his and a hint of a smile rose to her lips. "A detective with a sense of humor. I guess that's a twofer," she quipped.

Sean's forehead wrinkled slightly. "I have no idea what you're trying to say, but I'll just chalk it up to the shock talking," he said with a shrug.

She let out a long, shaky breath, then seemed to come to a decision. "All right, what can I do?" Orla wanted to know.

"Stay out of the way," he told her.

"To help," she clarified, clenching her teeth.

"Stay out of the way," he repeated.

"I know how to investigate. To put evidence together," Orla added.

"This was your father's *murder*," he emphasized. "I sincerely doubt if you know how to keep that separate—or to keep it from bringing you to your knees. If you really want to help, you just have to let me do my job."

Her eyes were shooting sparks at him. "You know, you really aren't an easy man to get along with."

He knew she was redirecting her anger at him in order to cope with what was going on inside of her. Sean decided that was fine with him. He didn't mind being a go-between in this situation. It was all part of the service that he offered in this sort of case.

"Never said I was," he told her.

Orla shrugged. "Well," she said philosophically, "at least you don't lie."

He smiled broadly at her, doing his best to distract her. "No, I do not. Now, if you're really bent on helping me…"

"Yes?" He could swear she almost sounded eager to him.

"Look around the apartment, see if anything is missing or was taken."

"That's a small enough request," she replied, scanning the area.

He nodded his acknowledgment of her assessment. "Yes, but sometimes it turns out to be the little things that wind up solving a case."

"Do you have an answer for everything?" Orla asked.

That was when his smile turned genuine on her. "I try, Ms. Roberts, I surely do try."

"Considering everything we've been through in the last hour or so, with you saving my life not being the least of it, I think that you have earned the right to refer to me as Orla—unless you find the name utterly off-putting," she told him. "At which point, you're free to use 'hey you' if you prefer."

He looked at her, somewhat puzzled. "You don't like your name?" The thought had never occurred to him one way or the other. He just thought of it as being rather unique.

"No, not really," she confessed.

He nodded. "Well, I'll be sure to keep that in mind."

Chapter 10

Although he certainly did not look it, in some ways, Sean Colton was the old-fashioned type. Rather than dictate notes into his cell phone, he found that he had a better chance of remembering the details if he wrote them down the old-fashioned way—by hand. Liam, Cormac and Eva all made fun of him for that, but Sean refused to change.

While making notes, Sean was careful to continue keeping an eye on the murdered real estate mogul's offspring, never once forgetting that Orla had very nearly become a victim of a hit and run. Though cars often sped in the city, he never believed that this could have been an accident. He could still feel the icy chill that had zipped down his spine when he saw the vehicle weaving almost directly at Orla.

To that end, Sean kept an eye on her, making sure that the other police personnel did the very same.

When he saw Orla stifling a yawn, he decided that was it for tonight. He didn't feel that he had to do everything himself. Sean gladly accepted input from others. He'd always believed that teamwork was the answer to solving crimes.

He glanced at his watch. It was late. Sean couldn't believe just how much time had passed.

"I'm calling it a night," Sean told the man who was working next to him. He assumed that if any of his siblings had made any headway finding out what had happened to Humphrey, he would have been notified.

He looked toward the last remaining crime scene investigator working the area. "I figure we can pick this up in the morning," he told Julio.

The older man nodded. "I was just about to suggest doing the same thing myself." He laughed to himself. "After a while, I find that my brain just stops processing things and all the facts start to merge into one overwhelming giant detail."

Sean nodded. "That's when I usually find that it's time to take a giant step back."

Flores laughed. "Amen to that."

Sean was beginning to feel punchy. "I'll touch base with you in the morning," he promised.

Flores stifled a yawn. "Just make sure it's not too

early," he requested. "My batteries really need to recharge. I'm not like you, Detective. I need to close my
eyes for more than just five minutes."

Sean's mouth curved. "You're exaggerating,
Julio."

Flores gave him a rather penetrating look. "Not by
much, Detective. Go," he said, waving in Orla's direction. The latter was sitting on a sofa, looking as if she
was fading. "Take your lady home. She's been through
a hell of a lot today," he empathized.

Overhearing the crime scene investigator, Orla
drew her shoulders back. "I am not his 'lady,'" she
protested, wanting to set the record straight. That was
just what she needed, to have the people the detective
worked with thinking they were a pair, or worse, that
she was attracted to him. He probably had a jealous
girlfriend—or maybe even a wife. "We just happened
to walk in together."

Flores retreated. "That might be the case, but that
doesn't change the fact that you *have* been through
a great deal," the man told her kindly. "Or that you
really look tired."

That changed nothing. Orla didn't want either man
thinking that she needed to be taken care of. The very
idea that she did would go a long way toward destroy-
ing her own self-image—not to mention his image
of her if it was even vaguely positive.

Orla pressed her lips together. She definitely regretted, in a moment of weakness, admitting to him that she needed protection.

Damn her sister, anyway!

The more she thought about it, the more positive she was that the driver of the black vehicle that had tried to run her down had been Aimee. Even though she hadn't seen the driver, she would have bet anything on it. Granted, she didn't recognize the vehicle, but Aimee could have easily stolen it.

It was definitely not unlike her sister, she thought.

Orla blew out an exhausted breath. Lord, she was weary all the way down to her toes. From what she could see, there was no end in sight.

She felt an arm around her shoulders and looked up, startled. "C'mon, we're going home," Sean told her.

"Whose home?" she asked suspiciously.

"I think you'll be safest if you stay in my place, at least for tonight. Although," he amended in the next breath, "probably for longer would make more sense."

She took umbrage at that. "I'm not a stray puppy that you picked up and need to take care of."

"No," he agreed calmly. "A stray puppy would undoubtedly be far more grateful."

Orla began to argue with the assumption he'd just made. But then, right in the middle, she stopped and laughed.

"I guess maybe you're right," she conceded.

"Does that mean that you're not about to continue giving me an argument about coming home with me?" he asked.

Orla nodded. "I'll come," she told him. "As long as you keep in mind that I am a martial arts instructor and not a damsel in distress."

His eyes met hers. Sean looked as if he was struggling to keep a grin off his face. He inclined his head. "I consider myself forewarned," he told her.

Ordinarily, she would have locked horns with him over what she perceived as his flippant attitude. But instinctively, she sensed that he didn't mean anything by it. If anything, the detective was going out of his way—*far* out of his way—to humor her at the very least. For whatever reason, she couldn't work herself up to get annoyed with the man. Not to mention the fact that she didn't even have the energy for that.

It was as if she was trying to outrun her thoughts. If she stopped long enough to allow her thoughts to catch up to her, to embed themselves deeply in her head, she would wind up falling apart. And if that happened, she was afraid she just wouldn't be able to pull herself together.

Another thought took her prisoner.

Her father was dead.

They were never going to be able to talk, to resolve any of the conflicts that were still left outstanding in their lives. But she had really wanted to try.

Her mother could only find fault with everything she did. Orla got the distinct impression that her mother was prouder of Aimee. Even when Aimee had been convicted and sent to prison, her mother seemed to think that that was Orla's fault.

Orla had been able to commiserate with her father over all the grief that Aimee had caused both of them.

Orla felt a sadness wash over her. That wouldn't happen anymore.

I'll get her, Dad, Orla silently promised again. *If it's the last thing I ever do, I'll get her.*

"You've gotten awfully quiet," Sean noticed as he escorted her out of her father's building. "I didn't actually manage to intimidate you, did I?" he asked her with a laugh.

The question surprised her. Orla began to give him an accusing look until she realized that he was trying to kid her out of her silence. That was when she told him, "I was just thinking about my father."

"I am very sorry about that. I know what it's like to lose a father. To lose both parents, actually," he said. "Even when you know it's coming—which we did because Dad had cancer. You can't really be prepared for the toll it winds up taking on you."

Reaching his destination, Sean drove into his building's underground garage and pulled into a numbered parking spot. Coming to a stop, he applied the handbrake. "I am so very sorry for what you're going through," he told her again.

She shrugged, doing her best to keep a tight rein on her emotions. She knew that if she loosened her hold even slightly, she would dissolve into a huge puddle of tears and this time, she might not be able to recover. That did not go with her super-tough image.

So she waved away Sean's apology, staring past his head. "It's not your fault my sister finally got her wish and did away with our father. Had you gotten here just a little earlier, you might think you'd have been able to prevent her from doing away with my father—but she might have succeeded in killing you both."

Sean really doubted that could have been a possibility. He was extremely good at his job, but there was no point in telling Orla that. It would be like rubbing salt into her already painful wound.

What sort of a hateful child killed their own parent? he couldn't help wondering.

Orla's twin was obviously filled with hate.

"We're here," Sean told his passenger needlessly after she made no attempt to move or get out of his car.

Orla let out a long breath, nodding her head. "So I see," she responded.

She really looked tired, he thought. But maybe it would help her to focus on something normal. "We can still swing by your place and pick up something for you to wear tomorrow if you'd like."

Her expression hardened. "I'd rather not stop by my place right now. This will do fine." She held out her arms to display the outfit she had on.

"I can call my sister and ask her to go by your

place to pick up something if you'd prefer that," he offered.

"What I would prefer right now would be to drop the subject," she told him stiffly.

Sean inclined his head. He could see that she was struggling not to cry. "Consider it dropped," he murmured.

Getting out of his vehicle, he walked around to the other side. Opening the passenger door, he put his hand out to her.

It seemed as if Orla deliberately ignored his extended hand as she got out of the car on her own. Walking toward the exit, she approached the elevator. "What floor?" she wanted to know.

He half expected her to sprint up the stairs instead of getting on the elevator once he told her what floor he was on.

Sean could see that the distraught woman had just had a spurt of extra energy and was in the process of wondering whether she should risk attempting to burn it up. But he knew she would quickly wind up regretting it at this stage.

She was fading fast, he could easily see that.

"I'm on the third floor." He led the way to the elevator and pressed the button for it.

Once it arrived, he waited for Orla to get on. When she did, he pressed the number three. It arrived on his floor almost immediately.

Sean led the way down the hallway. There were

an equal number of apartments distributed on both sides.

"Not what you were expecting?" he guessed, judging by the expression on her face just after he unlocked his apartment door and pushed it open.

"My father is—*was*—" she corrected herself "—a real estate mogul. I wouldn't have expected your lifestyle to match his. Very few people's lifestyles ever did," she added. "My father liked to dazzle people and to impress them with how well he was doing in his life.

"At this point, my father had no real need for the money, but the accolades, well, that was a whole different story," she told him.

He gestured around his apartment. "This is undoubtedly nothing like what you're used to, but make yourself at home," he said, honestly doubting that she could.

Chapter 11

Orla slowly looked around. The detective's apartment appeared to be rather small, especially compared to her own, but given that it was a man's home—a busy man at that, it looked rather tidy.

She slanted a glance in his direction. "Cozy," she pronounced.

Sean smiled. "That's one word for it," he responded. With that, he told her, "You can have the bedroom, I'll take the sofa."

Orla didn't think that was very fair. She was a staunch believer in equality. "I'm not about to displace you," she protested. "From what I've managed to gather, you've put in as full a day as I have.

"Besides," she continued, still looking around, "I

never sleep all that well in a new bed for the first few days, not until I get used to the accommodations. By then, I'll either be back in my own place, or..." She shrugged, her voice drifting off.

Sean locked the front door, flipping both locks into place. "What's that supposed to mean?"

Orla gave him an innocent look. She was referring to the fact that Aimee might succeed in getting her, but she wasn't about to say as much. With another shrug, she told him, "Put your own meaning to it."

Sean looked at her as if he actually understood what she was suggesting, but of course he didn't.

"You are definitely an enigma, Orla, and I don't know if you noticed or not, but this mystery is already taxing enough without having a mental challenge thrown in on top of it."

"Sorry, I can leave," Orla said, her voice growing distant. She didn't like being lectured to, especially when she felt at such a loss, getting her true bearings.

"Or," he countered with a note of impatience, "you can straighten up and fly right."

Anger creased her forehead as she raised her chin. "I'm not accustomed to being spoken to that way."

"Obviously," he noted. "Maybe that's the problem."

Orla began to storm toward the door, intending to leave, but Sean caught hold of her wrist, holding her in place.

The look in his eyes did the same.

He backed off a little bit, perhaps realizing he had overplayed his hand.

"What do you say we have a do-over?" he suggested, then elaborated, "And start over again?"

For a moment, she debated giving him hell, then decided that he *was* going out of his way to protect her. Reading him the riot act would be an awful way to pay him back.

Orla blew out a shaky breath, then apologized. "Sorry," she murmured. "Where are my manners anyway?"

The question wasn't meant for him, but for herself. Still, he was the one who answered her. "Gone into hiding for the time being, it seems. That's okay," he told her. "You're entitled. I'm not here to point fingers, I'm just here to give you a place to find a little bit of solitude."

Usually she was the one who provided the solitude by either making her clients feel like they were safe, or assuring them that they would come out of this tailspin that either life—or some man they had mistakenly trusted—had knocked them into. She did not like feeling as if control of her life was completely out of her hands.

She felt a smile, grounded in gratitude, rising to her lips.

"I appreciate that," she said, voicing her feelings in a far more relaxed tone. "I know it doesn't sound that way, but I really do."

The smile he flashed her said he believed her. "No judgment," Sean told her. "The bedroom is right this way."

It was a small room, but, like the rest of the apartment, it was neat and clean and right now, she didn't require anything more than that.

But she felt guilty about taking over like this. "I still don't feel right about this," Orla confessed.

"Luckily there's no need for you to sign a document stating that you do," Sean quipped. "All you need to do at this point is just go along with it."

She gave him a dubious look, but she could see that he was really being sincere.

"Ordinarily," he continued, taking out a fresh set of sheets from the side closet and placing them on the bed, "I'd suggest that maybe you'd rather stay at my sister's place, but one of her rooms is being painted and although the smell of paint doesn't seem to bother her, it does bother most normal people.

"Can I interest you in having something to eat?" he asked her in a friendly voice.

Orla shook her head. "No."

"Okay, theme and variation on that question," he said. "When was the last time you had something to eat?"

Orla lifted her shoulders in response and then let them drop. To be totally honest, she couldn't really remember the last time she'd eaten. She vaguely remembered breakfast, but after that, she hadn't a clue.

Sean nodded. "That's what I thought," he murmured. "You do realize that it's important for you to eat something in order to keep going, don't you?"

She could feel her stomach rejecting the very idea of food. "Right now, if I ate something, I'm fairly sure that I'd wind up recycling it within minutes."

"Then we'll put something light into your system to keep that from happening. My late mother insisted that we put something nutritious into our bodies every day. She wouldn't allow us to leave the house until we did."

"Simple but wise," Orla commented.

"You would have liked her," Sean mused.

His comment surprised her. She wasn't accustomed to having anyone talking about their parent as someone they would have liked introducing her to. For the most part, she felt removed from people's day-to-day lives.

Until now, she thought.

She flashed a small smile at Sean, trying to imagine what his mother had been like. "I'm sure I would have," she said.

She could see that her response pleased him. Her smile grew a little wider.

Orla caught herself looking toward the refrigerator. Maybe, just for the sake of getting along, she should try consuming something.

"I'll have a piece of toast," she told him.

Sean immediately walked over to the refrigerator. "Well, it's a start," he said, taking out what was left of a loaf of bread.

Orla watched as the detective undid the twist tie that was holding the bag closed. "It's also a finish," she informed him.

He flashed a knowing smile in her direction. Now that she had left an opening, he was not about to back off. "You are nothing if not an optimist," he told her.

He was being sarcastic. She supposed that she really couldn't blame him. "This is all new to me," Orla admitted. "I was raised to be utterly conscious of the dark side. The lighter side is something I'm really not accustomed to."

Nodding, he said, "Maybe that's something we can work on once this is all behind us."

Was he planning on maintaining some sort of a relationship with her once this was over and they had managed to put her father's killer away? Orla wondered. It certainly sounded that way to her. Ordinarily, that would have gotten her back up, or at the very least, annoyed her.

Oddly enough, it didn't.

She couldn't begin to explain why, even to herself, but she did know that she was exceedingly aware that she'd caught herself actually smiling.

The toast had popped. Sean buttered it and placed the two slices of bread in front of her, then took a seat opposite her himself.

She noticed that the slices were golden brown and said as much. She hadn't told him how she liked it.

"You didn't strike me as a burnt toast kind of person," he told her. "But if this isn't to your liking, I can always make you something else. Just tell me what you prefer."

"This is fine," she assured him quickly. "Besides, I'm not about to have you jumping through hoops over toast. Especially since you were nice enough to insist on making it for me in the first place."

"I thought that maybe it would help you—us," he

corrected, "unwind." He smiled at her as he continued. "I figured that if I talk long enough, I might end up putting you to sleep—which is my ultimate goal."

She laughed as she swallowed the piece of toast she'd bitten off. "You're not *that* boring," Orla assured him.

"There might be a couple of people who would disagree with you," Sean told her.

"Your ex-fiancées?" she asked.

That was much too good a guess to just be a shot in the dark. He stared at her, stunned. "How did you..."

"I have my sources, even if I spend most of my time working." She had made a phone call to someone she knew while he'd been going over her father's apartment, looking for evidence, but there was no reason for her to admit to that.

"There is a reason why they became exes," he said. "They didn't appreciate competing with my line of work. As a matter of fact, they resented it."

"I never had that problem. For me it was strictly work," Orla admitted.

"Spending too much time that way could be taxing for anyone. You need to unwind, to relax," he told her, adding, "to learn to breathe."

Orla looked at him knowingly. "Said the police detective who rescues hit-and-run targets in his spare time."

He smiled, probably catching the intended irony. "Hey, we all have to have hobbies to help us cope with the stresses of our job," he told her. He glanced down at her plate and nodded with approval. She'd finished the toast, every last bit of it, rather than leaving some of the crust behind. "You cleaned your plate. Want more?"

"Oddly enough, maybe one more slice," she answered. Saying that, she waved him back to his seat. "You stay put, Detective. I can make it myself. I'm not exactly a great cook," she freely admitted. "But I assure you, I can handle making toast. It doesn't exactly require a gift—or even mild expertise." She laughed.

He gestured toward the toaster, indicating that she should go ahead and make the toast.

As he watched, she put in two slices.

"Do you feel like talking?" he asked her as the two new slices popped.

She looked at him, somewhat confused. "I thought that was what I was doing," she said, puzzled.

"No, I meant talking about your father and what you're going through with your sister. Actually, about anything at all," he amended.

He waved at her. "Never mind, carry on." He flashed a rueful expression at her. "As you can see, I'm really not very good at small talk or getting people to unburden themselves."

"I have no need to unburden myself," she said, bringing the plate back to the table. "If I did, I would have availed myself of a psychiatrist. All I need is a warm body to talk to. If that makes you uncomfortable…" Her voice trailed off.

"I didn't say that," he told her. "I also don't want you to feel that I'm attempting to interrogate you."

Orla nodded her head. "Tell you what, no preconceived notions, how's that?" she asked.

The smile he sent her way managed to warm her heart with no effort at all. "That suits me," Sean responded.

Orla talked until she realized that her eyes were closing.

Sean saw her head drooping down and then over to the side.

"Looks like my company *is* putting you to sleep," he noted with a soft laugh.

Sean gave Orla another fifteen minutes, then very slowly, he rose from the sofa. For a moment, he debated letting Orla go to sleep that way, then decided that by the time morning arrived, she would have one killer of a crick in her neck. One that would take her more than a day to get over.

Very gently, he slid over and then picked her up in his arms. Executing very careful, gentle steps, Sean carried the sleeping woman into the lone bedroom.

He kept his eyes on her face the entire time, worried that in her present condition, if she woke up now, she might find his carrying her into the bedroom as some sort of breach of trust. Most likely, she might even think that he was up to something.

Still watching her face carefully, he placed Orla on the bed, then covered her with the comforter that he kept gathered up on the edge.

She began to stir and he froze; then very slowly, he resumed moving until he was finished covering her.

Something stirred within him, a gentle feeling that he ordinarily reserved for a very small circle of people in his life.

He was just tired, Sean thought.

"See you in the morning," he told her softly. Making his way back toward the sofa and the living room, he stopped dead when he saw Rockwell Roberts's face on the TV screen.

Obviously the story had broken. He had hoped they'd have more time to work the case before it went public. It looked as if tomorrow was going to be one very busy day. He'd better get his rest now while he was still able to do so—if he was going to be of any use to her tomorrow.

Before he lay down on the sofa, he shut off the TV. The last thing he wanted was to wake up to a "breaking news bulletin."

He was asleep in moments.

Chapter 12

Orla was certain that she would wind up tossing and turning for the remainder of the night. Instead, to her unending surprise and relief, she found that she wound up sleeping a lot better than she'd imagined she would.

She didn't exactly wake up fully rested by a long shot, but she *had* slept for several hours.

When her eyes did flutter open, it was in response to the aromatic, tempting scent of coffee, scrambled eggs and toast.

Since she had fallen asleep in the clothes that she'd worn the night before, she had no need to get dressed: she already was.

Sitting up in bed, Orla scrubbed her hands over

her face, doing her very best to come to. She had no recollection of walking into the bedroom and lying down, so she was fairly certain that she had been carried to bed. Not only that, but apparently Sean had covered her with a comforter as well. She had no idea whether or not to mention that to the detective, or just pretend she hadn't noticed any of it.

First things first, she thought, getting up and slipping on her shoes, she went to the bathroom, threw water into her face and brushed her teeth. She began to feel a little human. At that point, she followed the very tempting scent of coffee as well as the breakfast that Sean had prepared, to its source.

She leaned against the doorway, taking the scene in. Apparently he'd just finished with the preparations.

"That smells wonderful," she told him.

Surprised, he looked over his shoulder as he set the plates down on the table. He waved off her compliment. "That's just because you really haven't eaten anything in hours."

She had never met a man so determined to shrug off any sort of compliment. Joe, the former boyfriend who had caused her so much grief, had a head one and a half times the normal size and liked to pound his chest any opportunity he got, she remembered. It was that trait that had caused her to become introverted.

"I'm pretty sure that the smell of burnt food, or something akin to that, would have completely turned me off. This, however," she said as he placed the plate in front of her, "smells absolutely wonderful." She looked at Sean pointedly. "Learn to take a compliment, Detective," she told him.

"I could say the same thing to you," he pointed out, sitting down at the table opposite her.

She inclined her head in acknowledgment of his comment. "Touché, Detective." Taking a healthy forkful, she slipped it into her mouth. "This is really good." Orla looked up at him. "Who taught you how to cook?" she wanted to know.

"I picked it up by watching my mother when I was a little kid. Then I found I had to do it in earnest when Mom got sick because my father was too busy working around the clock to pay for my mother's bills. When she passed, I was still cooking for my siblings because my father was dying of cancer. He was too sick to do anything."

Orla took the information in in awed silence. "You're a pretty impressive man, Detective Colton," she commented.

Sean didn't see it as being a big deal. "You do what you have to do," he said.

"Don't downplay it. It's not as common as you might think." Finished eating, she picked up her plate as well as his. Sean began to get up to take the plates from her.

"One doesn't have to have a special talent to wash dishes," she told him. "Trust me, if there was, there would be a huge stack of dishes piled up all over my place." She glanced at the open laptop that was sitting on the counter. She couldn't help wondering if the news media had said anything about what had happened to her father. Most likely, the story about her twin and that hateful boyfriend of hers—she certainly wouldn't refer to him as *her* boyfriend—had probably already made the rounds.

"Do you mind if I turn on the TV?" Orla asked even as she was making her way over to the monitor in the living room. She grabbed the remote before he had a chance to answer.

Immediately, the image of her slain father was all over the screen. It was a twenty-year-old picture that showed him at his best.

"The newest version of 'Poor Little Rich Girl' is on everyone's lips," the announcer was saying. "Real estate tycoon Rockwell Roberts was found dead in his Manhattan apartment sometime yesterday morning. According to CSI crew who were sent to the scene to conduct an investigation, Roberts's daughter's DNA was found to be all over the premises. Speculation is that Roberts's daughter Orla grew tired of waiting for crumbs to be tossed in her direction and decided that it was high time to claim her inheritance now while she could enjoy it."

Stunned, she turned away and looked at Sean, completely indignant.

"How could they say that?" she demanded, outraged. "They didn't even bother mentioning Aimee as a possible suspect. Even though her escape from prison was everywhere, I would've thought that would be the first thing the news media jumped on. Don't they bother to vet their stories from moment to moment?"

"Obviously not," Sean replied. Crossing to the TV, he was about to shut it off, but she caught his arm, stopping him. He raised his eyebrows, an obvious question in his eyes.

"Leave it on," she told him. "I want to hear what they have to say."

"No, you don't," he insisted. "There is absolutely no reason to get aggravated. These people are sensationalists. The more they stir people up, the bigger their audience is. Tomorrow there'll be another story to grab people's attention and this will be old news."

Orla frowned. "I'm not all that sure," she said. "A lot of damage can be done in a very small space of time."

"By then," Sean told her confidently, "we'll track down your sister and that guy she fled prison with and arrest them."

She turned toward him at the same time she turned off the TV set. She'd heard more than enough. "Then you believe me?" she asked.

"Yes," he answered. "I believe you."

That should have been enough for her, she thought, but it wasn't. She was afraid to believe *him* and she said as much.

"Why?" she asked. "Why do you believe me?"

"Because I saw the look in your eyes. Because I

saw how very broken up you looked when you saw your father's lifeless body on the floor."

Something prodded her to provoke him. "You know, I could have just been acting," she pointed out.

"You could have," he allowed. "But I tend to trust my gut. And my gut tells me that you really cared about your father, more than you could possibly put into words." He looked at her pointedly. "But out of sheer curiosity, why are you insisting on playing devil's advocate?"

"Maybe because all my life, I've been anticipating the worst happening. It's better to be prepared than to be devastated."

"I can understand being prepared, but then when do you leave yourself time to be happy?" he asked her.

"Simple. I don't," she answered. But then she rethought her response. "Actually, my work makes me happy. Every time I manage to save a woman from being abused and learning how to stand up for herself, I feel very, very satisfied with the career path I've chosen."

"That is a very admirable path," he agreed. "But there has to be a little personal happiness in there for you."

"This is enough for me," she told him.

At that point his cell phone rang. He held up his hand, stopping her from saying anything further. "Sorry, I have to take this."

Orla gestured for him to go ahead. "Don't mind me," she said.

* * *

Sean turned his back toward Orla as he walked to another part of the room. Only then did he answer the call.

The caller was his captain. An image of the attractive, blonde-haired woman instantly popped into his mind.

"Colton," he answered.

"Colton, this is Captain Reeves," the voice on the other end of the call announced, "Where did you leave it with Roberts's daughter?" she asked.

The question threw him. "Excuse me, Captain?"

"You said that you felt she needed her own protection detail. Did you get one for her?" his boss wanted to know.

He decided that it was best to remain vague for the time being until he knew where this was going. "Orla Roberts is a very stubborn woman," he told her. "She resists any offer of help." Which was true because she had initially turned down his offer to act as her protective detail. "What's up, Captain?"

He was not expecting her response. "I'm debating having you arrest her," Reeves told him.

Sean put some more distance between himself and his houseguest. He didn't want Orla accidentally overhearing him until he managed to resolve this situation. "Why would I do that, Captain?"

"Because I think she might be behind her father's murder," the captain answered bluntly.

Rather than protest and go directly to Orla's defense, he asked, "What would be her motive?"

"The oldest reason in the world," Reeves told him. "She was looking to inherit a rather huge fortune."

He didn't need any time to think his answer over. "I don't think she's guilty. As a matter of fact, I'm willing to bet absolutely anything that she's not."

"I've never known you to make a snap judgment, Colton," the captain said.

He didn't ordinarily cite this when he spoke to his superior, but this felt different somehow. "Just call it a gut feeling," Sean told his boss.

"I'll hold off putting any labels on it for now." She paused for a moment, then asked, "Tell me, does this 'gut feeling' of yours extend to the other twin as well as Aimee's lover? They both escaped from prison at the same time. What's to keep all three of them from throwing their lots in together and splitting the money?"

When she heard Sean hesitating in his response, she made another guess. "Another gut feeling?" she wanted to know.

"Something like that, Captain," he agreed.

"Just what did Orla Roberts say to you?" Reeves wanted to know.

"It wasn't exactly what she said, it was the way she said it, the way she presented herself," he explained to his superior. "I am willing to bet my job that this woman did not do anything to even endanger Roberts's life, much less end it." He paused for a moment, then told her, "I have a very high score when it comes to being right about certain things."

"All right, I'll go along with you for now. But know that it's subject to change, Colton."

"Yes, ma'am," he replied solemnly. "I never doubted that possibility."

There was silence on the other end of the line, a great deal of silence, to the point that he almost suspected the woman had hung up on him. And then, in a quiet voice, Captain Reeves told him, "All right, I believe you, Colton. That gut of yours has been right more times than my own instincts have been. Prove her innocent, or show me someone else who's guilty of the crime. Otherwise..." Her voice trailed off.

He knew what she was saying and he would take what he could get.

"Understood, Captain," he told her.

He knew he had been put on notice.

Chapter 13

"What was that all about?" Orla asked when Sean closed his phone and came back into the kitchen.

He shrugged, wondering just how much of an excuse Orla would be willing to accept. He had no doubt that her radar was up. Being who she was, she had to be used to people lying to her.

Or, at the very least, exaggerating a great deal.

"That was just my captain being extra cautious," he explained.

Orla was silent for a moment, as if she was trying to read between the lines. "Captain Reeves thinks I'm the one who killed my father, doesn't she?"

She seemed rather unusually calm to him as she

made the guess. Sean couldn't help thinking that Orla was just attempting to protect herself.

He also knew that lying to her would definitely get them off on the wrong foot. "Let's just say that right now, she's not quite sure what to think," Sean told her.

"I can understand that. In her position, I wouldn't know what to think, either. Unless they have a history of being abused, women don't take to me right away. But women who've been abused sense I can relate to them."

Sean looked at her, surprised. She was the last person he would have thought that about. The words emerged before he could stop them. "You've been abused?"

"It was a long time ago—before I had any brains."

From her expression, he got the feeling she hadn't really intended to tell him about it, that it had been a slip of the tongue. Compassion stirred within him. "Do you want to talk about it?" he asked her.

"No," Orla answered flatly.

"Fair enough." Although he felt she would have been better off talking about it and getting it off her chest, at least to a small degree.

But he'd already learned one significant thing about her. Orla Roberts could not be pressured into doing anything that she didn't want to.

"All right, what do you want to do?" he asked.

Orla was barely paying attention to what he was

saying. Her mind was clearly elsewhere. "My father's at the morgue right now, isn't he?" she asked Sean.

"Yes," he answered slowly, wondering where this was going. "Why?"

"Can you take me there?" she requested pointedly.

"I can," he replied. "Any particular reason why you'd want to go by the morgue?"

Orla took in a deep breath, as if to brace herself. When Rockwell Roberts had been alive, this would have never even crossed her mind. But her father was no longer among the living and never would be again.

She swallowed hard and then uttered the words. "I'd like to say goodbye without any gawking people around."

Sean knew that had to cost her. He didn't want to draw the moment out. "That can be arranged," he told her. "When do you want to go?"

"As soon as possible. Hopefully before anyone figures out where I'm staying. Unless you think people already know that I'm staying with you," she said. And then she switched directions. "Is it all right if I shower here?"

"Sure." And then he paused before deadpanning, "There'll be a slight charge."

Orla stared at him. "You're kidding."

Obviously, a sense of humor was the first thing to go in this sort of situation, he thought.

"Yes, I'm kidding. It's called trying to lighten the moment up. I guess I'm not very good at it," he admitted. "Homicide doesn't allow me to get much practice at this kind of thing."

Orla offered the detective a half smile in response, apparently realizing he was attempting to be nice.

"I appreciate the effort," Orla told him.

"It was nothing," he said, then underscored, "*Really* nothing."

She nodded, hurrying back to Sean's bedroom for a moment. "I'll be ready in a few minutes," she promised before Sean handed over towels.

Sean couldn't get over how weird all of this felt, he thought. He had never been abrupt with a victim's relative, but he had never gone out of his way for that relative, either, he thought, as he washed and dried the breakfast dishes as well as the frying pan.

Turning around, he almost dropped the tiny stack he had gathered up. Looking refreshed and neat, Orla was already out of the bedroom.

"Wow, you weren't kidding about finishing quickly," he marveled.

"Well, you're going out of your way for me. I didn't think it would be exactly fair to make you wait for me to get finished."

His eyes swept over her to make sure she was ready. She was, he thought. "I didn't even get a chance to make sure that the dishes were completely dried," he said. "Well, since you look as if you're ready, let's get going."

They made their way back down to his underground garage.

Orla kept her head down as they crossed paths with several people that Sean obviously knew. She waited until they were well past those people. "Friends of yours?" she asked.

"Neighbors," he corrected. "It's always a good thing to keep communication with neighbors open," he told her. "You never know when one of them might wind up telling you something."

Reaching his vehicle, Sean opened the passenger door for her, then waited. She slid in and he closed the door behind her.

Inching forward in what felt like stop-and-go traffic, he glanced in her direction. "You're being awfully quiet," Sean noted.

Orla had receded into her own little world, totally oblivious of doing so. She took in a long breath before answering. "Just bracing myself for what's to come," she told him.

"When you go see your father in the morgue, do you want company?" he asked. He had learned quickly not to assume anything when it came to Orla.

And he was right.

"No," she answered. "This is going to be the last time that my father and I 'interact' so to speak. I want to do it alone."

He didn't know many women like her, Sean thought.

"Totally understandable," he replied. "I'll take you down to the morgue and then step outside. You can take as long as you need. When you're done, just come out. I'll be waiting in the hallway."

Still seated in his vehicle, she turned to look at him. "You're being awfully nice," Orla commented. It sounded as if it wasn't the kind of thing that she took for granted.

"You've read my résumé," he responded with a laugh.

Sean was no mind reader, but it looked as if his humor was having the intended effect. Not that she'd ever admit it.

Right now, all she could manage to say was, "Thank you for that."

He glanced at her innocently. "I have no idea what you're talking about," he told her. And then he grinned at her and winked.

Somehow, putting the woman at ease just felt like the right thing to do. He got the distinct feeling that she had been put through a great deal for most of her life. It was time to cut the woman some slack.

Being born to wealth wasn't quite the picnic it was cut out to be, Sean mused.

After parking his car on the ground floor of the precinct, Sean made his way through the building with Orla at his side. Eventually, he brought her to the morgue.

There was a solemnity that all but vibrated throughout the morgue. It could be felt all the way down to the bone. At least that was the way that Orla felt.

The medical examiner was sitting at his desk, filling out his latest paperwork. Whatever he was working on had his full attention, and it took the mild-mannered examiner a couple of minutes to become aware of the duo's presence in the room.

"Is there something I can help you with?" the man asked the two of them. And then he took a second look as recognition sank in. "Detective Colton, I didn't realize it was you for a minute. Do you need anything?"

"No, not me, but Ms. Roberts—" Sean nodded toward Orla "—is requesting a few minutes alone with her father. If it's all right with you," he added. "Orla, this is Dr. Bruce Crawford."

The ME's gray eyes moved back and forth like a fully wound-up metronome, moving from the woman with the detective to a drawer located on the back wall. "I thought he looked familiar when Mr. Roberts was brought down yesterday. I'm still waiting on the paperwork," he informed Sean. "You have my deepest sympathies, Ms. Roberts," Dr. Crawford told Orla with utter sincerity.

"So is it all right for her to say her goodbyes in private?" Sean asked the medical examiner.

Dr. Crawford moved to the back wall and then gestured toward the drawer he opened for them.

"Of course," he said, then encouraged her to "Take as long as you need."

"Thank you," Orla murmured, moving toward the drawer.

"Is there anything I can get you?" the medical examiner wanted to know.

"Just some privacy," Orla replied. She wasn't looking at either man in front of her. Her attention was fixed on the figure that was draped with a sheet and lying on the gurney. She was almost afraid to lift the sheet.

"Of course, of course," the medical examiner responded, already moving toward the door leading out into the hall.

"I'll be waiting right outside the double doors," Sean told Orla. She knew he was probably violating protocol by leaving her alone with the body, but she appreciated his kind gesture.

With that, he followed Dr. Crawford through the doors leading out into the hall.

Alone now, Orla stood there, draped in silence for several minutes. She absorbed the significance of the moment, that this was going to be the very last time she was going to be standing like this in her father's presence.

Orla could feel the tears gathering in her throat, making it very difficult for her to breathe. With effort, she pushed on, making herself form words.

"Oh, Dad, there are so many things that are left unsaid, so many conversations that we're never going to have," she lamented. "If we had to do it all over again, I'd like to think we would have both done things differently.

"I wouldn't have been so angry at you for letting Aimee get away with so many things just because you felt guilty about favoring me, and maybe you—" several tears slid down her cheeks "—maybe you would have been able to see me for the person I was instead of the person that Aimee actually turned out to be."

Orla stopped talking for a moment, her voice breaking as her tears once again welled up to fill her eyes.

She wasn't going to embarrass herself, even alone, like this, she silently lectured. She wasn't doing herself or the memory of her father any good by behaving this way, Orla thought sadly.

Using the back of her hand, she rubbed away her tears. Taking a deep breath, she held it, then let it out slowly as she looked down at her father's still face.

"I know you always tried to go softly on Aimee because on some level, you felt it was your fault that she felt so slighted, so inadequate, but it wasn't. None of it was. We all spent too much time taking the blame for things that were Aimee's fault, not ours. With all my heart, I wish we had that time back so we could just spend at least a little of it with each other and not in that special hell that Aimee created for all of us.

"You were always so busy, creating that empire of yours. I never really got to know you, except for the way you felt about Aimee," Orla whispered. "You applauded her victories, however minor they actually were, and just ignored mine. I thought that the only way I could get you to love me was to be tough and independent."

She threaded her fingers through her father's very cold ones. Orla shivered a little as the temperature registered.

"I'm so sorry that this happened to you. Sorry I was so oblivious to everything, I didn't see it coming until it was too late to stop it from engulfing us. If Aimee was involved in this in any way, Dad, I promise that I will make her pay."

Orla stood there in silence, her heart aching to the point that it was almost painful.

"Aimee and that pathetic excuse of a male specimen," she told her father, calling up an image of her former boyfriend, the man who had escaped prison with Aimee. Aimee, though, was definitely the person who had masterminded this whole thing, she thought.

Orla laughed under her breath. If she was anything even mildly like Aimee, she wouldn't allow herself to feel guilty at all.

Instead, she felt completely consumed by waves of guilt and it was utterly her twin's fault.

From the bottom of her soul, Orla once again promised revenge.

Then her eyes shifted back toward her father. "You'll have that funeral you always wanted, Dad. I promise."

She was wasting time talking to a man who couldn't even hear her when she was alive. Orla did her best to snap out of the downward spiral his death had sent her into.

Moreover, she was wasting time, time she could be spending searching for her sister, she thought, clenching her fists.

"See you on the other side, Dad," she told the figure on the gurney.

With that, Orla straightened her shoulders and marched over to the morgue's door to summon the detective.

Chapter 14

Sean saw Orla coming toward him. Straightening up, he immediately made his way over to her.

"Did you say everything to your father that you wanted to say?" Sean asked, joining Orla.

Her laugh was dry and totally devoid of any humor. "I didn't even cover half of it," she admitted, "but then I didn't think I would."

He looked at her, surprised. "Then why did you come out of the morgue? There's no reason for you to stop talking to your dad if you have something left to say."

This time her smile was genuine. "I said every-thing I felt actually needed to be said. I could have gone on talking indefinitely," she admitted. "But there was really no point to it." Her tear-filled eyes met his. "I said everything to my father to clear the air."

Sean nodded. "I guess you can't ask for more than that."

She raised her eyes to his, a half laugh lingering on her lips. "Oh yes I can," she contradicted him. "For one thing, I can ask for Aimee's head to be on a pike."

He knew that Orla really believed that her twin sister was guilty of their father's death. Quite honestly, so did he. But believing and being able to prove what he believed were two very different things.

"All in good time," he promised. "If she's guilty—"

Orla interrupted him, insisting vehemently, "She is."

He didn't bother to argue with her about that. It was pointless. "Well, then we'll prove it."

She frowned as they walked to the elevator. Sean pressed the up button. "You're just humoring me," she muttered.

"Well, actually yes, I am," he agreed. He saw the surprised look cross her face. "But that doesn't make it any less true," he pointed out.

Orla frowned slightly. "You're treating me like I'm a kindergartener."

"Would you be happier if I argued with you over this? If I fought you at every single turn?"

Orla frowned. "No," she admitted.

"Then I think you need to make up your mind about how you want this to go," he told her.

She shook her head. "When did life get so complicated?"

The same question had occurred to him more than once, especially in the last few days. There still hadn't been any news about Humphrey, even though his brothers and sister were still attempting to track him down. "The minute you opened yourself up to it."

She frowned again. "All I had to do was place one foot in front of the other and go from here to there. That's just not the case anymore."

Sean thought of his own life. Nothing about it had ever been simple, but somehow, despite everything, he and his siblings had managed to reach their goals and accomplish things. And they all felt they were honoring their father by becoming part of law enforcement. He and Eva had wanted to become part of the police department, so, despite all the obstacles they'd encountered, they did manage to accomplish their goal.

As for the twins, Cormac and Liam, the two couldn't have been more different from one another. At least not to begin with. Cormac wanted to be his own boss, so rather than join the police force where he would have to listen to and take orders from someone who very possibly had an inflated ego, he became a private investigator.

On the other hand, Liam, was an ex-con who had actually served time for a while before straightening up and opting to run a juvenile awareness program for the NYPD. He had done that by becoming part of a team, but at bottom, he was still very much his own man.

And all of them had done this in memory of their father.

"Sometimes we wind up with more than we bargained for," Sean told her. "Look, I have some details to take care of. Why don't I drop you off at my apartment? That way, you can stay safe while you recharge. I think you could do with the rest."

Her expression suggested she didn't like that idea. "I've worked for most of my life. It was the one thing that my father liked most about me," she said in all sincerity. "I'd rather not be forced to abandon that aspect of my life. Vegetating was never my style.

"Besides," she continued, "the people who were associated with my father will be expecting a big funeral. My father knew an awful lot of people from all walks of life. I'm the only one who has access to his various address books and can invite them to his funeral. My father would be horrified if any of these people were overlooked. He would have considered it a slight."

Sean looked at her. "No offense, Orla, but your father's gone. I really doubt that who's invited one way or another would make a difference to him at this point."

But Orla remained firm and shook her head.

"Appearances were everything to my father," Orla insisted. "There's no reason to believe that fact has changed just because my father is gone. At this point, it's a given."

He stared at her. This wasn't making any sense to him, "What does that even mean?" he wanted to know.

"You don't need to know the answer to that," she told him matter-of-factly. "All you need to know is that it was true for my father."

He sighed. "Whatever makes you feel better."

"I owe him that much," she said.

Sean had learned a long time ago that a person's beliefs were a very private matter that in general could not be interfered with. The upshot was that he would only be asking for trouble if he tried to get her to change her mind. It was wiser to just drop the matter.

"Fine," he responded agreeably. "Just let me know where and when," he told her, "and I'll alert the members of the force. But you'll have to wait for his body to be released. It's evidence in a murder investigation."

"Okay. I'll let you know as soon as I get in contact with St. Patrick's Cathedral."

That stopped Sean dead in his tracks. "You plan to hold this in St. Patrick's Cathedral?" he asked her, surprised.

"Yes." The way she said it, it didn't sound as if she considered it to be a big deal.

"Do you have any idea how long the waiting list is for a funeral to be held at St. Patrick's?" he asked her, stunned.

She looked completely unfazed. "My father was very aware of the problem, which is why he prepaid for the funeral, also adding an extremely generous amount on top of the usual sum—which wasn't exactly a tiny pittance. Trust me, as soon as the story broke in the news today, the church has been waiting for my phone call about finalizing the arrangements," she said sadly.

"That must have been a very hefty donation," Sean commented.

"Oh, it was. It is," she assured him with emphasis. "My father was never known to do things in a small way."

"Obviously," he agreed. "All right, let me make a call to my superior, updating her about this latest development, and then I'll drive you over so you can talk to whoever you need to see at St. Patrick's."

Orla held up her hand, stopping him. "That's very generous of you, but I'm not exactly helpless here. You do what you need to do, and I'll catch a cab to St. Patrick's to talk over the details that are involved in my father's funeral. We can get together later if that makes you feel better."

"What will make me feel better," Sean said, "is if every detail that's raised between us doesn't turn out to be a tug-of-war."

She looked at him, her eyes widening. And then she laughed softly. "If you think that *this* is a tug-of-war, you have definitely led a very sheltered existence."

"Well, call it whatever you want," he informed

her, "you're still not going to St. Patrick's to make any arrangements without me."

She would have thought that Sean would welcome her trying to take care of things on her own, rather than falling back on him and utilizing him as if he was her unofficial babysitter.

"You're actually serious?" she asked in disbelief.

"Completely and utterly." Sean gave her a long, penetrating look that she supposed was meant to put her in her place. It failed. "Look, you might enjoy risking your life or playing death-defying games because on some level, it will make you feel less guilty about your father being killed, but I'm not going to be a party to that. It happened, I'm very sorry it did, but my job includes the need to keep you alive," the detective told her.

"Funny, you said your captain told you that she was trying to make up her mind as to whether or not to have you bring me in and, oh yes, have me arrested for my father's murder," she added flippantly.

Granted she had never heard anything so ridiculous in her life, but there it was, a completely baseless accusation. It infuriated her beyond words because she had never even been seen arguing publicly with her father, much less threatening him with any sort of bodily harm.

Though he hadn't said anything to her about it, Orla was fairly certain that the detective had checked that accusation out and found it as ridiculous as she had.

"For the time being, I convinced Captain Reeves that you had nothing to do with it," he told her.

She knew it, Orla thought with satisfaction. Her eyes met his and she smiled at him. "You are a good man, Detective Colton."

"That's part of my job description," he fired back.

Orla nodded. "All right, then let's go to St. Patrick's so we can get started making those funeral arrangements."

Sean looked at her. "This might sound very naive," he granted, "but don't you need to make an appointment before you get to see one of the priests at St. Patrick's about your father's funeral?"

"Since the story about my father's murder broke, I am assuming that Father Scanlon is expecting to have me come in as soon as possible."

"Of course he is," Sean answered with a sigh. "All right, let's go," he encouraged, bringing her over to his vehicle. He opened the door for her and waited for Orla to get in on the passenger side.

St. Patrick's Cathedral was located at Fifth Avenue between Fiftieth and Fifty-First Streets. As usual, traffic proved to be quite heavy, the way it normally was at almost any given hour of the day within the heart of the city.

Parking was trickier, but he did manage to find some, then waited for Orla to make her way out of his vehicle.

"Okay," Sean told her, "this is where you take over. You lead the way from here on in—unless of course, you don't know where to go," he theorized, waiting for her to say something.

She explained that she'd only met with Father Scanlon once. It had been an introductory meeting, laying the groundwork for the inevitable, sad "someday." Given that her father was the picture of health and actually looked years younger than his actual age, it was easy to see why her father and the priest felt that the inevitable "someday" was years off in the future.

A very efficient-looking, thin woman in her late fifties brought Sean and Orla into Father Scanlon's office. Busy making notes, the thin man pushed them aside and was instantly on his feet. Exuding warmth, Father Scanlon crossed over to them and took Orla's hands into his.

"Oh, my dear, please accept my deepest sympathies on the unexpected death of your father. Rockwell Roberts was a wonderful man with an exceptionally generous heart and by all rights, he should have lived many, many years longer instead of being so abruptly robbed of all that time," the priest genuinely lamented.

Sean could see that, faced with the priest's sympathy, Orla was once again fighting back tears.

"I totally agree, Father," she told the middle-aged priest.

His expression was kindness personified. "I assume you're here to finalize your father's funeral arrangements?" he asked.

She nodded, and Sean could hear her struggling to breathe normally. "The sooner the better."

"Of course, of course," Father Scanlon quickly agreed. "Have any of your father's directives changed since he initially had them drawn up?"

"I see no reason for his directives to have changed," she replied. "I would like to hold the funeral as soon as possible."

Fear was gnawing away at the pit of Orla's stomach, though she tried mightily to prevent that fear from showing on her face. She wouldn't put it past her twin to do something drastic that would somehow disrupt the funeral.

As much as she dreaded having to sit through the actual service, she really wanted to put all of this behind her and move on.

She knew she wouldn't be able to draw a normal breath until her father was finally laid to rest. After that, she felt that she would be free to deal with Aimee.

Chapter 15

If she wouldn't have to pay for the destroyed television monitor, Joe knew Aimee would have thrown a rock dead center through the set or found a way to throw the television set across the room right now.

"How dare the bitch?" Aimee shouted angrily at the screen, pacing back and forth. She was consumed with fury.

Joe knew that tone. If it wasn't for the fact that the woman was exceptionally handy to have around—she was the one who had come up with the escape plan, not to mention the money that was more than sustaining them—he would have dumped Aimee a long time ago.

Oh, who was he kidding? She scared him. Aimee might have been rich, but she was also dangerous and crazy. Joe didn't trust her any further than he could throw her. Her other attributes—as well as her gorgeous face and figure—had long since lost their appeal for him.

In addition to which, he knew he couldn't risk angering Aimee. He was confident that the woman could turn on him in an instant and he no longer knew exactly what she was capable of.

Right now, she was yelling at the television set— and at the person who wasn't there. "What's she done now?" he asked, being careful not to sigh. He was totally weary of her drama and her behavior. He didn't like taking chances and if it had been up to him, they would have been gone by now.

But he also knew that if he attempted to walk out on her, the unpredictable woman could easily turn around and kill him.

Aimee's eyes were flashing as she continued pacing around the room. Her anger wasn't abating, it was mounting. She spun around to face Joe.

"What's she done?" Aimee echoed. "I'll tell you what she's done. She's holding a big, fancy funeral for the bastard. And it's at St. Patrick's Cathedral," she spat out.

Joe shrugged, not seeing what the big deal was. "Well, he is her father." Joe pointed out.

Aimee glared at her lover, furious. Her eyes were shooting daggers at him. "Are you defending that little bitch?" she demanded hotly.

That was his signal to back away. "I'm not standing up for her," he protested. "I'm just stating the obvious."

"Yeah, well, maybe I don't feel like listening to the obvious," she snapped at him hotly. "Ever think of that?"

"I get that," he said, lowering his voice. "Why don't we just blow this place?" As far as he could see, that would be the logical solution.

"What, and have her think she chased me away? Not on your life," Aimee all but shouted into his face.

Joe shook his head. Despite what the woman was saying, her twin was *not* all-seeing. "She doesn't even know we're still in the city," he argued. "I wouldn't have assumed that if I was in her place."

Aimee laughed nastily. "That's why you're *not* in her place," she told him. "Orla knows. Oh, she knows. You forget, we've got that twin-radar going."

Joe frowned, feeling his temper growing as it slipped through his fingers. Aimee might have been incredibly hot in bed, but she had the ability to make him lose his patience faster than the speed of light.

He also knew that she would immediately cut off his head if he ever said anything to that effect. Still, he just couldn't keep himself from commenting.

"That twin-radar is just a myth."

Aimee became highly indignant. "No, it's not, Joe. It's real. Very, very real," she insisted. "Don't ever think that it's not."

He glanced up at the news story regarding her father's upcoming funeral. The man was dead and he was still making Aimee crazy, he thought.

"It'll all be over with soon," Joe promised the woman who had become his meal ticket.

"But meanwhile, she's preening around, enjoying being the center of attention—*again*," Aimee spat.

"Yeah, but you were the one who got to kill him," Joe reminded her.

The thought momentarily brought a satisfied smile to Aimee's lips as she apparently gloried in the memory. "Yeah, I was, wasn't I?" And then the smile vanished as if it had never existed. "We need to get rid of her."

It made no difference to him one way or another. What did make a difference to him was the possibility of getting caught. Staying one step ahead of Aimee was exhausting.

"We will," he assured Aimee, hoping that would placate her for the time being. "First thing we need to do is come up with a plan."

Aimee's expression turned ugly. Now what? he couldn't help wondering.

"Do I have to come up with *everything*?" she demanded.

"Of course not. We just work better when we work together," Joe told her in a quiet, mild voice, trying to calm her down.

For the time being, that seemed to mollify her, he thought, relieved.

* * *

Orla felt that she had to proceed with caution to ensure that her father's funeral did not turn into some sort of three-ring circus. She wanted the funeral to be conducted tastefully and respectfully, honoring all the things that her father had accomplished. Orla was proud of the fact that her father was not someone who took advantage of the people he sold property to. So many people weren't.

"You know, I don't remember things being so complicated and involved when it came to my father's funeral," Sean told Orla. "But then, Uncle Humphrey handled all the details."

She looked up from her laptop she had placed on Father Scanlon's desk. She'd been inputting all of her father's friends and associates, being very careful not to forget anyone. Appearances had been everything in her father's world.

For a second, her mind had temporarily gone blank. "How old were you at the time?" she asked Sean.

"Eighteen," he said.

That was right, he'd told her that, she remembered. "That had to be rough."

"It would have been rougher if Uncle Humphrey hadn't been there," Sean said.

His thoughts turned toward the man. Taking care of Orla and helping her was taking up all his time right now, so he had put the matter of finding Humphrey into his siblings' hands. They had reached out to their cousins, FBI agent Deirdre Colton and US marshal Aidan Colton to keep them in the loop, but so far they hadn't needed their assistance. He hoped they'd find Humphrey before his cousins needed to be brought in.

"Uncle Humphrey took care of all the details, paid for the entire funeral and put us up in his building. Don't know what any of us would have done without him," he told her.

"I'm keeping you from that investigation," she realized. "That's not right. I don't need you to hold my hand," she assured Sean, not for the first time.

"No, you need me to guard you and watch your back. You're forgetting how close you came to being roadkill," he reminded her. "Next time, that person—" he was assuming it was her twin, although this time, he left her name unsaid "—just might succeed. And don't give me that garbage about being able to take care of yourself."

She pressed her lips together, looking as if she was trying to hold her tongue.

His tone lightened. "How's it going?" It couldn't be easy for her, notifying all those people about her father's funeral services. He had seen enough funeral services to know that if she wasn't careful, it could go completely astray.

An ironic smile played on her lips. "There is no way that this will wind up being a small, tasteful service. Best I can hope for is that this doesn't turn into a media extravaganza."

"Are you planning on saying any words over your father?" he asked her.

He could see by the look on her face that until that moment, she hadn't been planning on it. She paused now, thinking over Sean's question.

"I guess I'll have to now," Orla answered.

"You don't have to if you don't want to," he pointed out. "After all, there's no one forcing you."

Orla shook her head. "Wrong. *I'm* forcing me," she told him.

He thought over what she'd said. "I'm behind you no matter what you decide to do."

His words caught her off guard. She studied him and realized that he really meant what he said. Odd though it seemed, it gave her something to hang on to.

Her smile reached her eyes. "I really appreciate that, Detective."

"Sean," he told her. "My name is Sean."

Orla nodded, amending her statement, "I really appreciate that, Sean."

They smiled at one another and the rough, choppy seas momentarily abated.

Orla felt, at least temporarily, that their relationship had taken a turn for the better. For the first time since she could remember, she didn't feel alone and adrift, trying to cope with all the curves she had been thrown for years now.

Thinking back, she really couldn't remember the last time she hadn't felt alone and adrift. But the loneliness had eventually enabled her to learn how to stand up for herself as well as learn how to terminate an abusive relationship.

Once she'd freed herself from her own abuser, the very least she could do was to pass this ability on to the women who came to her, looking for help.

She changed the subject for now. "I guess you'll be coming with me to the service."

"You guessed correctly," he responded.

"And until then…?" she asked, wondering what he had in mind.

"I'll be stashing you in my apartment," he told her. "Unless you'd rather stay at my sister's place."

She didn't feel up to dealing with a new set of circumstances. "I've gotten used to intruding on you," she said.

"Good, then we'll keep things the way they are. I'm fairly certain that your twin doesn't have the resources to find out where I'm staying."

Orla smiled at him. *Let's hope not*, she thought. Out loud she said, "My money's on you."

He waited until she finished with the lists of participants she was busy drawing up.

Beyond exhausted, Orla rose from the desk Father Scanlon had vacated for her. She immediately had the detective's attention. He was on his feet instantly.

"I'm just going to go find Father Scanlon to tell him I am done for the day," she explained.

Sean nodded. "I'll go with you."

"You don't have to," she told him.

"Oh yes I do," he contradicted.

Orla stared at him, surprised. The man couldn't be saying what she thought he was saying.

"Nothing's going to happen to me here," she insisted. "This is a *church*. And it's not *just* a church. This is St. Patrick's Cathedral, for heaven's sake. *St. Patrick's Cathedral*," she stressed again with more than a little emphasis.

But Sean shook his head. "That doesn't make you safe," he insisted. "Church doesn't mean anything to the people we're dealing with, not even St. Patrick's Cathedral." She was walking now and he followed less than a step behind her. "Let's go and tell Father Scanlon you're coming back tomorrow to finish up. Does that sound all right to you?" he asked her.

At this point, Orla felt as if her eyes were crossing in front of her. "Absolutely," she assured Sean.

They found the priest waiting for them. It was as if the man knew to expect them.

Orla made her arrangements and then they left shortly after that. She was surprised when he took her straight home without stopping for food. She took that to mean that he wasn't hungry.

It wasn't until he brought her into his apartment that she detected the enticing scent that seemed to be pervading through every nook and cranny in the apartment, whetting and stirring her appetite.

"What smells so good?" she wanted to know.

"Dinner," he told her. "I had Eva pick up a meal to go a little while ago. I think if I didn't keep track, you wouldn't eat anything at all and would just wind up wasting away."

She laughed softly as she walked into his apartment. "To be very honest, at this point, I think I'm hungry enough to start eating the furniture."

"Luckily," Sean said with a grin, gesturing toward the take-out bag standing on the table, "you won't have to."

Chapter 16

Orla let out a deep, satisfied breath as she looked down at her now empty plate. "That was very good," she told Sean.

"Glad you liked it," he said, putting away the rest of the leftovers. "There's more if you're interested." He nodded at the container he was about to store in the refrigerator.

"Breakfast," she replied. "I couldn't eat any more right now. I'll wind up exploding."

Sean laughed softly. "Wouldn't want that," he told her. "For one thing, I'm in no shape to clean up anything right now."

"I wouldn't let you," she said. "Not after everything

you've put yourself through for me. That just wouldn't be right."

"What 'everything'?" he asked, feigning innocence. "I just took you in to protect you." His eyes met hers and held. "Not exactly a huge hardship."

"Don't act so innocent. I heard you arguing with your superior."

"That wasn't an argument. I just raised my voice because she's hard of hearing," Sean explained.

She gave him a look that said she didn't believe a word of what he was saying. "Uh-huh. And if I asked her about her so-called hearing problem?"

"She'd break both of your legs, but that's just because Captain Reeves wouldn't want to emphasize her shortcomings." He said it with such conviction, she could almost believe him.

Almost.

But she knew he was just making things up for her benefit. In hindsight, this man who was dealing with so many demands on his time, was treating her far better than anyone in her family ever had.

The whole situation made her feel exceedingly vulnerable. She was accustomed to not just doing things for herself but also not needing to rely on anyone else for emotional support.

She felt a stab of guilt as she upbraided herself. She should have been here to take care of her father. She knew what Aimee was capable of. The moment there had been even the slightest hint that her twin had escaped from prison, she should have immediately sent someone to protect her father until she could get to him herself.

She could feel tears beginning to clog her throat again. Ever since Aimee had managed to escape from prison, killing those two guards, Orla had felt this overwhelming regret washing over her, regret she couldn't seem to be able to get a handle on.

When they were very young, one bitterly cold winter they had gone to play on the frozen lake. The ice made a terrible noise as it suddenly cracked beneath their feet.

Orla, always the fast one, had managed to make it to dry land but Aimee, frozen in fear, watched as the ice began to crack on all sides of her. Orla remembered hearing her sister's bloodcurdling scream for help. Orla never even paused to think about the danger. Instead, she laid herself flat on the ice and managed to inch her way back just in time to wrap her hand around her sister's wrist. Holding on as tightly as she could, she dragged Aimee back to safety.

If she hadn't been as fast as she was in managing to pull Aimee to safety, none of this would have happened. Not the death of the guards and especially not her father's murder.

The world would have been far better off if she hadn't been as quick as she was.

But she knew that if she hadn't been able to save her twin, there would have been a wave of regret accompanying that as well.

She let out a shaky breath. Damned if she did and damned if she didn't.

Sean returned to the table after loading up the dishwasher with the plates that he had just rinsed off.

The sight of Orla's tears seemed to stop him in his tracks.

"Dinner not to your liking?" he cracked, obviously trying to kid her out of her frame of mind.

The question was so absurd, it succeeded in making her laugh. Laugh so hard that once she started, it was hard for her to catch her breath and get herself to stop.

"No, you big idiot," she finally sputtered.

"Then what?" Sean asked in a mildly interested voice, trying to redirect her focus.

She'd be willing to bet her answer was not one that he would have expected. "I'm regretting saving my sister." His tone never changed. "I wouldn't have wanted you to do that," he said.

"Why?" she wanted to know. The way she saw it, Aimee had created nothing but problems for all of them.

"Because if you killed your twin, I would have had to arrest you and bring you in," he told Orla. "Nothing would have made me more unhappy than to have to do that."

"Maybe *kill* isn't exactly the right word," she qualified. "But when we were younger, I saved her life once. I'm thinking maybe I should have let her die. If I had, my father would still be alive. I wouldn't have minded being arrested. As far as I'm concerned," she continued, "that represents a very decent trade-off."

"But if you killed her, you would have been sitting in prison," he reminded her. Sean put his hands on her shoulders and drew her closer. Very gently, using the corner of his thumb, Sean wiped away the tracks of her tears. "As painful as it is to acknowledge, things do have a way of working themselves out."

She looked at him. Both of his parents had died, first one, then the other and his siblings came dangerously close to being raised as wards of the state. And yet, amazingly enough, the man had devoted himself to law enforcement and he could still think the way he did.

There was no question about it, the man had an exceedingly strong character. For that matter, it seemed like his entire family did, being dedicated to some aspect of law enforcement the way they were.

Orla took a deep breath, telling herself that if Sean could do that, could think that way after what he'd been through, well then, so could she.

Raising her head, she tried to muster a smile as she looked up into those beautiful green eyes of his. "I guess I should be looking to you as an example," she told him.

Sean seemed to be fighting some inner battle. He finally forced a smile to his lips. "I guess, until you find someone better to look to—and that isn't really difficult—I'll let you," he allowed.

Orla couldn't begin to put into words how exceedingly grateful she was to this man. Sean Colton made her feel safe, made her feel that there was still hope that things could ultimately turn out to be all right.

She honestly couldn't remember being the one who made the first move. For one thing, it wasn't the sort of thing she did—ever.

But she felt herself being completely drawn to this man, desperately vulnerable and wanting to connect with him. One moment, she felt her heart pounding hard enough in her chest to crack her ribs, the next moment her lips were pressed against his, trying to make him understand just how very drawn to him she was.

Orla didn't think past the moment, because the moment was all there was—and all that there really needed to be.

She felt the depth of the kiss growing, and she sank into it. There seemed to be no bottom to it, she thought as it occurred to her that she'd never felt like this before. Not even when she fancied herself in love with Joe, the only man she had ever gone to bed with.

Orla now realized that that feeling was nothing like the one she was experiencing here at this moment with Sean.

Damn but Orla had gone and lit a fire in him, Sean thought. A fire that was all but consuming him. A fire that he couldn't allow to get the upper hand over him. He wasn't the sort who normally took advantage of the rules or bent them just to suit his needs.

And yet, his attraction to this woman had made him forget all that. He could feel a hunger growing inside of him to almost mind-boggling, overwhelming proportions.

Sean kept telling himself to just keep on kissing her a little while longer. All he wanted was just to continue feeling this rapture a few more minutes.

But he was well aware where that sort of path led—to places he couldn't allow himself to visit. Not safely. Even a second longer might completely prevent him from turning away from where he knew he was inevitably heading.

So when she rose up on her toes, pressing her body urgently against his as if her very life depended on it, Sean removed her arms from around his neck and held her in place. "Orla, I can't," he whispered.

He expected that would be enough. That she would step back, seeking refuge from the rejection and creating a wall between them.

But apparently she just couldn't.

Instead, she pressed her body against Sean's and began to weave a continuous braid of kisses along his face, his neck and along the space where she had undone his shirt.

"Sure you can," she whispered in a husky voice. Orla breathed heavily as she continued to rain more kisses along his body.

Sean couldn't explain, even to himself, why he didn't just push her away. Why, instead, he allowed this to progress to the stage where he found himself undressing her even as he allowed her to undress him.

Still exchanging kisses and breathing more and more heavily, he wound up stumbling with her into the bedroom, fanning flames that he had managed to convince himself he could easily walk away from.

He knew he was lying.

There was *no* walking away from this.

Sean could feel her heart pounding against his chest and that just excited him and made him want her all the more.

What had happened to him?

Why couldn't he walk away? For his own good? For hers?

But he couldn't, not even if she placed dynamite between them.

The pounding of his heart all but immobilized him.

What the hell was happening here?

He had no answers, he realized. And no weapon against the way she was making him feel. Without even trying, she had managed to bring him to his knees—literally as well as figuratively.

The network of kisses he wove along her now-nude body had her twisting and turning, desperate to absorb the sensation.

Seeking more.

Why had they had to meet under these circumstances? She made him feel a way he never had before and he went out of his way to ensure that this feeling was mutual. Because, when the threat from her sister was finally over, he intended to take this thing between them to a whole new, different level, one that wouldn't have her worrying that he had ulterior motives.

Sean didn't have to ask her any questions to know that a woman with her family background had been pursued all her life, mostly with the emphasis on her money.

He had no actual use for money beyond what he earned. He did, however, have a really huge use for the way she made him feel.

And he intended to convince her of that no matter how long it took.

With soft, breathy kisses, Sean blazed a trail of moist desire going up and down her body until she all but melted into him, urgently twisting and turning against him.

When he finally entered her, making their two, pulsating bodies into one, he lost all sense of time and place.

It took him a while to finally descend to earth and longer than that to get his heart to beat normally.

He noted, with no small satisfaction, that Orla didn't return to normal immediately, either.

Gathering her in his arms, Sean held her against him. The beat of her heart felt oddly soothing, another new sensation for him, he thought.

"Well, that was a surprise," he murmured against her forehead.

"Which part?" she asked, making herself comfortable against him.

He felt her breath tickling his chest. "All of it," he said, laughing at himself more than at the situation.

"What's so funny?"

"Me," he said. "This."

She shifted a little to be able to look up at him. "I'm going to need more than that to make sense out of this," she told him.

"Until just now, I would have said that I was a cop with a will of iron." Tilting her head up so that her eyes met his, he said, "You just proved me wrong."

Orla sat up and searched his face. "You regret doing this?"

He grinned at her. "Not in a million years."

She sighed, content as she lay back down into the cradle of his arms. "Good," she whispered. "Me neither." And then something he had never seen before in relation to her, a look of mischief crossed her face. "Want to do it again?" she asked.

He knew he would regret it. A full day stretched before him when he got up in the morning. But he wouldn't be able to live with himself if he walked away from enjoying a second round.

"You know, I think I'm going to need to stock up on vitamins—big-time," he said before bringing his lips down to hers again.

Chapter 17

The moment Sean slipped out of bed, Orla's eyes flew open. Subconsciously, part of her knew that the easiest way for her to proceed would have been to pretend to go on sleeping until he left the room. She instinctively knew that the moments after lovemaking for the first time were always the hardest to deal with.

But she had always believed that facing up to things was the most honest way to go.

"Hi," Orla murmured, drawing the comforter up against her as she sat up, watching Sean walk across the room.

He was focusing so hard on being quiet, she had startled him when she spoke. But he managed to recover quickly.

"Sorry, I didn't mean to wake you," Sean murmured.

"You didn't," she freely admitted. "I really wasn't sleeping."

Sean sat back down on the edge of his bed. Somehow, moving quickly, he had managed to slip a pair of boxers on between their lovemaking and his getting out of bed.

He cleared his throat now, as if stalling for time. Finally he spoke. "Um, look, if I wound up making things uncomfortable for you somehow. That definitely was not my intention."

"Well, you succeeded in getting your intentions across, because that wasn't my perception of what was happening." Moved by his sensitivity, Orla slowly stroked his cheek. "I was the one pursuing you. Actually, what happened between us—when it happened—amounted to excellent timing." Sitting up straighter, she tucked the drooping sheet up against her.

"Now, how do you want to divide this up?" she asked, temporarily losing him until she elaborated. "Shall I take care of making breakfast while you shower, or vice versa?"

He apparently hadn't expected her to say that and he laughed, relieved. "Actually, since I already broke the cardinal rule about having a relationship with someone I was in charge of guarding, I was thinking that maybe we could indulge—temporarily—in more of the same."

His breath was warm on her face and she could feel all these stirrings going on within her, responding to him.

She kissed him then, but when he leaned in to continue what she'd started, she placed her fingertips on his lips, drawing her head back. "I'm supposed to be at St. Patrick's first thing this morning to finish up with the funeral arrangements," she reminded him.

Sean let out a long, weary breath. "I remember," he answered quietly. "All right, why don't you go ahead and take that shower while I make breakfast."

She nodded, rising from his bed, the sheet tucked loosely around her body. "All right," she agreed. "You talked me into it."

He laughed softly. "Happy to do it," Sean responded wholeheartedly.

They were at St. Patrick's within the hour.

While Orla spent the next few hours sitting within the office, talking to the priest as well as finalizing the names of the people who had made the cut and were being invited to her father's funeral services, Sean was busy on his own cell phone coordinating the search for exactly what happened to his father's best friend.

Thank goodness he could count on his brothers and his sister to work on that. He owed it not just to Humphrey but to Humphrey's wife as well. After all, he had promised her that he would find the man. Not just do his best to find him, but actually *find* him.

People did not just vanish into thin air without a trace, not even in New York, he reasoned, and certainly not men as famous in their field as Humphrey Kelly was in his.

And deep down, he knew that if he had an extra moment to spare, he needed to use that to find who had killed Lana Brinkley, that sweet-faced young woman whose case he had been originally assigned. He'd reluctantly given the case over to Mitch Mallard, NYPD partner of his sister Eva, who was a bit of a blowhard. Sean wasn't happy about it, but there was no way he could continue to give Lana's case the full attention it needed.

Sean was still beyond certain that Wes Westmore, the man Lana had been living with, was the one who was responsible for stealing that life away from her.

Somehow, in the four and a half minutes that he had left over at the end of his day, he was going to have to find definitive proof what he felt deep in his gut was the way that things really happened.

But in the meantime, coordinating the efforts of his three siblings and assigning them to different phases of the search for Humphrey, took up more of Sean's time than he would have imagined. He was also trying to stay abreast of any new developments that might have taken place.

In that light, he could just imagine what Orla had to be going through with conducting her father's funeral arrangements on such a grand scale. It made Sean silently promise that when his time came, he wanted a simple service to be held with his ashes scattered to the winds at the end of it.

Estimating that he had given her enough time to finish up, Sean walked back into Father Scanlon's office and over toward Orla. "You looked wiped out," he commented.

"I just never realized that my father had so many friends, acquaintances, business associates and who knows who else to sort through. Just getting through the list and consolidating it is a hugely monumental task."

"Why don't you call your mother or your father's lawyer and ask them for help?" Sean suggested.

She answered simply, "Because I don't ask for help. I can handle this. Besides, I know my mother. She would say something to the effect that he finally couldn't embarrass her anymore." She saw the expression on the detective's face and guessed what was behind it. "She wouldn't kill him, but she's not about to cry that he's gone, either."

Sean just shook his head, silently marveling. "Nice to know you're not stubborn."

Her lips just slipped into a smile. "I was wondering when you would catch on to that," she teased.

"So, are you all set, then?" he asked her. "I'm sure that Father Scanlon would see his way to extending the date that you had initially selected. He looked like a very kind, reasonable man or priest or however you're supposed to refer to him."

"He likes the term *priest* or *father*," she told Sean.

"And he is—*very kind,*" she emphasized. "I've known him ever since I was a little girl."

"So the funeral service is going to go off on time?" Sean asked, wanting to confirm the fact.

She looked at Sean as if his suggesting otherwise had to be a poor joke on his part.

"Yes, it'll go off on schedule—tomorrow," she confirmed. "My father would never forgive me if it didn't."

He looked at her, wondering if she was serious. "I don't think that your dad is in any position to hold a grudge," he told her.

The laugh she emitted was unexpected, he thought. But then he reconsidered, maybe it wasn't. Orla, he was beginning to realize, was totally unpredictable.

"You obviously don't know my father."

"No," he agreed. "I never had the pleasure."

She cocked her head, as if thinking over his phraseology. "That's one way to look at it." Switching subjects, she informed him, "The services will be held at ten o'clock tomorrow."

"I'll let the captain know," he told Orla. "I'm going to need to give her a copy of the guest list so she'll know just how many people she's going to have officers watch over and keep safe."

When she and Sean finally called it a night and went back to his apartment, Orla noticed that there were several police personnel planted in various places within the building.

"Kind of crowded," she couldn't help commenting.

"That's just to ensure that you don't find yourself missing the service because of something that your twin caused," he told her.

Orla laughed under her breath. Sean was good, she thought. "You are catching on, Detective."

"That's because you're rubbing off on me," he said, leading her into his apartment.

She looked around her. His people had to know that she was staying in his living quarters. "Aren't your people going to talk?" she asked.

He shrugged. "They'll talk anyway," he assured her. "But if it makes you uncomfortable, I can have someone else guarding you—or have you stay somewhere else."

Orla shook her head at the suggestion. "I'd be uncomfortable if I had someone else guarding me." The fact that this was going to be her father's funeral all but echoed in her head. "As it is, I doubt if I'm going to be able to sleep," she told him.

"Why don't you just take it one step at a time?" Sean suggested. "If sleep comes, great. You can think of it as a bonus. If it doesn't come, I'm sure it probably won't be the first time."

The man had a laid-back way of looking at things that she found soothing, she thought. He knew his stuff and she found that his approach had a way of taking the edge off.

"You're right. It wouldn't be. There was a point

when getting an hour's worth of sleep would have been a fantastic bonus," she recalled.

Taking a deep breath the next morning, Sean let the scent of Orla's hair weave its way through his system. He smiled to himself.

He had his people scattered throughout the building as well as the surrounding blocks. He was taking no chances on anything happening to her—and definitely not on his watch.

Sean still woke up early, letting Orla sleep until 6:30 a.m. He had a feeling that she wouldn't forgive him if he allowed her to sleep longer than that.

Orla managed to get ready very quickly. He found himself amazed.

His eyes carefully traveled over the length of her, taking every single inch into account. She took his breath away. Orla was wearing a black colored two-piece suit with matching three-inch heels.

Damn but she looked beautiful, he caught himself thinking. "That outfit suits you," he commented appreciatively.

Orla hadn't been going for his approval, but upon hearing it, she had to admit that it really felt good. Mostly, it made her feel that she was not alone. Being alone was the way she'd spent a good deal of her life, estranged from her mother and her sister and only fleetingly connected to her father.

It suddenly occurred to her that she had to be extra

careful not to allow herself to get too attached to Sean. After all, what was she to him, really? She was his latest assignment, nothing more, she reminded herself.

Once her father was laid to rest today and Aimee didn't appear to surface—and at the moment, she felt on instinct that wasn't likely to happen—Sean would just move on to his next assignment. An assignment, she was well aware, that wasn't going to have anything to do with her.

"I'm glad you approve," Orla told him, slowly turning all around in front of him.

Sean laughed softly at the comment. "I'd have to be blind not to."

How was it that in the midst of all this ongoing sorrow washing over her, this detective could still make her feel good? she wondered. She had no answers, only questions, but at least, she thought, because of him she was alive to form these questions.

A woman whom Orla knew from pictures to be Sean's sister Eva, suddenly peeked into her brother's apartment. "Ready to go?" she, clad in her dress uniform, asked. The question was directed at Orla, not at her brother.

Orla nodded. "Unbelievably ready," she confirmed.

And she was. She was incredibly eager to put all this behind her because only then would she be able to grieve in peace.

Taking her comment in, Eva nodded. "Then let's go," she urged. "We've just undertaken and completed another clean sweep of the area. For the moment, it would seem like all systems are a go."

"All right, then, let's go," Orla said, nodding toward the door.

She was trying her very best not to notice how the words she'd just uttered seemed to be sticking to the roof of her mouth.

Sean nodded at her, giving Orla the crook of his arm to hold on to.

When she took it, he guided her out of the apartment using slow, precise steps.

Chapter 18

St. Patrick's Cathedral was an impressive structure when there was no one in the building. When there were throngs of people practically filling up every space within the 143-year-old building, the way there were at the present moment, it was exceedingly over-whelming.

There were so many people in the cathedral now, there seemed to be hardly any room within it to move around and breathe.

Orla scanned the area, thinking of her father. He had spent a lifetime trying to advance himself, but he also did attempt to serve his fellow man and woman and was determined to do right by them.

I guess they appreciated it, Dad. You would have been happy to see this.

He would have also been surprised to see her mother amid the people "paying their respects." Orla hardly ever saw her mother these days. Months would go by without a word. But she would have bet anything that the woman wouldn't have missed the funeral. Not because her mother had any feelings for the man she had married, but because she liked being in the public eye. She was wearing an expensive black designer suit which flattered her curves. The news media ate it up and the woman knew it.

Halfway through the lengthy service, Sean leaned over toward Orla and whispered, "How are you holding up?"

She looked at him in surprise. He couldn't have said anything kinder or more thoughtful if he'd planned it. Doing her best not to show how affected she was by his question—after all, they were out in public with cameras pointed at them—mainly her—from all different directions, Orla still felt truly touched.

Her lips quirked in a semi-smile. "Holding my own," she whispered back.

It was a long service, with a lot of people stepping up to the front to say kind things about her father, which they may or may not have meant, but for the moment, it still warmed her heart. The general public had been allowed to form a compassionate picture of her father. She was grateful for that, though she'd decided not to speak publicly as she'd planned to.

And when the entire service was finally over, Sean put his arm protectively around her shoulders and with his brothers, sister and several of the people from the department he worked with running interference for them, he kept Orla protected and at the very center of this movement. She felt comforted by his presence and the way he was able to guide her safely out of the crowded church.

Once he had deposited Orla into his car, Sean sat back for a moment, probably catching his breath.

"All right," he said, "where to now? There isn't a reception planned, I know."

Orla never hesitated. She was that convinced that she was right. "Now I help you track down my sister so she can be made to stand trial for what she and Joe did to my father."

He seemed a bit surprised by her response, but he didn't say what he was thinking.

"My guess is that they would be long gone from here by now," Sean finally told her.

"Why? To their way of thinking, they got away with the crime of the century and besides, they're not about to walk away from the money they feel is coming to them, even if it is in a bank in the Cayman Islands."

"They risked a great deal for freedom," was the way he saw it.

"No," Orla contradicted, "they risked a great deal

to get what they—at least Aimee—felt was coming to her. I guarantee that my sister is not about to go anywhere until she gets her hands on it. In case you missed it, my sister has a very inflated sense of self."

"So in the meantime, until this gets resolved, you're going to be wandering around with a target on your back?"

Orla squared her shoulders. "If that's what it takes to resolve this and capture Aimee, then yes, I will have a target on my back."

He frowned as he looked at her, desperately wanting to talk some sense into Orla. There was no getting away from the fact that, without even trying, he had managed to fall for her. He was not about to ignore that.

But he wasn't about to just rubber-stamp what she was planning on doing. "I can't make up my mind if you're being exceedingly loyal to your father—or just exceedingly stupid when it comes to carrying out vengeance. No offense," he added.

"Well, if I get a vote in this, I'll go with choice number one," Orla told him.

Sean nodded. "I thought you might, but me, I'm not all that sure. You do realize that Captain Reeves is still thinking about arresting you for being in on your father's murder."

"But you made her see the error of her ways, right?" she asked.

"I'm working on it," he said. "But bringing Aimee

and her boyfriend in would go a long way in getting our point across." He was convinced Orla was innocent and that her heart was in the right place. As much as he believed in her, however, he knew his boss would need more solid proof.

"I think that maybe we should set a trap for Bonnie and Clyde," Orla began. "I could—" She didn't get a chance to finish.

Sean's face immediately clouded up. "No, no, no!" he declared. "There will be no setting up any traps on your part. I'm not about to have you turn into some sort of live bait. There just has to be another way," he said. "In the meanwhile, I'm planning on keeping you close—not that I don't trust you, but I don't," he told her plainly. "In the meantime, I'm sending the CSI team back to your father's apartment to do another deep search. Maybe they missed finding a set of your sister's prints that had been left on the scene."

"You haven't found them yet," she pointed out.

"That doesn't mean that we won't," he said stubbornly. "Things happen. It's a big apartment, and your sister is definitely not a fool. She didn't exactly run around, wiping her fingerprints off every single surface she came in contact with." He paused as he finally started up his vehicle. "Did she show up at your father's residence very often?"

"He didn't exactly mention it," Orla told Sean. "But then, I didn't keep tabs on what my father was doing. He had his world, I had mine. Occasionally, he would tell me what Aimee was up to. When she and Joe were arrested for stalking me two years ago, I thought that Aimee would stay put, at least for a while."

Visibly upset, Orla pressed her lips together as she looked away. "I should have never let my guard down."

He could hear the wave of emotion she was struggling to contain. His heart went out to her. "You know, this wasn't your fault," he told her.

Orla must have realized what he was trying to do. "Saying so doesn't make me feel any better. It also doesn't change anything."

Coming to a stop, he glanced at her. "You're not going to find any peace until you learn to forgive yourself."

"Since when did they make psych courses part of the required background that a detective brings to the job?" she asked.

"It's not required," he told her. "It's just something I managed to pick up along the way. I'm a quick study and Uncle Humphrey all but oozed the stuff when he talked to us. This was, granted, before he got married, but that still amounted to over sixteen years worth of education."

He glanced at Orla as he got to the point of all this. "Now that the funeral is over, I need to get back to looking for Uncle Humphrey. We've got videos of him walking into the courthouse, but then nothing. He never came out. The man couldn't have just disappeared into thin air," Sean insisted, frustrated.

Orla shook her head. "For one thing," she said, thinking of the photograph he had shown her, "the man is just too big."

Sean found himself being grateful that Orla wasn't referring to Humphrey using the past tense. Yes, he had to admit that was a rather small thing, but at the same time, it did make him feel somewhat better. By not using the past tense, it made Sean feel as if the psychiatrist was still very much among the living.

"Do you need help?" she asked suddenly.

He wasn't sure how she could help.

"What do you mean?" Sean asked.

"I'm asking you if you need help looking for Humphrey Kelly?" she explained. "I really need to feel useful right now and you just said you don't want me laying a trap for Aimee, so this is the only other thing I can think of doing at the moment."

He had another solution for her. "You could pick up where you left off teaching those self-defense classes and showing abused women how to protect themselves," he told her.

"And you want me to do this with you hovering around?"

He hadn't taken that aspect of it into account, Sean realized. He was still on protective detail when it came to her. "You have a point," he acknowledged.

"I know," she told him. "I do have a brain," Orla stressed, then added, tongue in cheek, "I'm not just another pretty face."

Midtown traffic was incredibly slow. Sean's eyes managed to hold hers for a long moment.

"No," he agreed, "you're not. You are a very specific, unique pretty face."

"I wasn't fishing for a compliment," she said.

The smile managed to make its way to his eyes. "I know."

"And besides, any compliment you give me perforce fits my sister as well."

"I'm afraid I'd have to argue with you on that score," he said, thinking of a clip he had seen of Aimee's prison escape. "Your twin's eyes lack a soul, which makes the two of you look completely different," he told her.

Orla's smile grew wider. "You do have a way with words."

"You inspire me," he said.

"Something tells me I should quit while I am ahead," Orla muttered.

"Why don't we continue this discussion later on—in bed?" he suggested.

She smiled. "Works for me."

Orla wasn't fooling herself. This relationship between them did not have the mark of "forever" about it, but she planned to make the very most of it and enjoy it to the nth degree for as long as it lasted.

They arrived at his apartment and she was prepared to get down to work in an attempt to clear her mind of what had just transpired. But Sean had another idea and told her as much, deliberately being vague.

"All right, then," she said agreeably. "Lead the way."

But rather than walking, he told her, "I've got another idea."

And Sean suddenly scooped her up in his arms and in a matter of moments, he was carrying her into his bedroom.

Delighted, feeling all the tension momentarily leeching out of her body, Orla wove her arms around his neck and gave herself up to living in the moment. She had just learned the hard way how few and fleeting those moments could be. That meant they could be utterly gone within the blink of an eye.

Her heart was racing madly as Sean carried her into the bedroom and lay her on his bed. Orla focused on that and nothing more, rejoicing in the way that Sean made her feel.

Tomorrow it might all change, she knew that. But now, following her father's burial and living in the moment that had been created by all those kind, respectful words that had been said about her father, Orla was singularly focused on making love with Sean and enjoying doing that to the nth degree.

They made love several times until, exhausted, they both fell asleep.

When morning arrived, Orla's normal inclination to bounce out of bed, something she had been doing every morning for her entire life, stalled to the point that she found herself curling up into Sean's body. It was a very nice feeling, she caught herself thinking, for him to be with her as his siblings were looking into Humphrey's disappearance.

She was really reluctant to get up.

Catching hold of his shoulder—despite this being the dead of winter, and neither one of them were wearing anything beyond a satisfied smile—she pulled him back to her.

"Stay," she whispered seductively in his ear.

He raised his head, a quizzical look in his eyes. "I thought you told me that you were an early riser."

"I am. Normally," she answered.

"But not today?" he asked.

Her smile spread out along her lips. "Not today," she replied. "At least, not just yet."

"Not just yet?" he echoed, raising himself up on his elbow so that he could look down into her eyes. "Then what is it that you do want to do first thing this morning?" he asked her.

Orla was very aware of the time and knew exactly how much she had to spare. Just enough to get her engine running, she thought. She moved, centering herself until she was beneath Sean. Reaching up, she took his face into her hands so that she only had to raise her head up just a little bit more in order to plant her lips directly against his.

Her breath moved seductively against his lips, just out of reach.

Her eyes met his, holding him in place. His question echoed in her brain.

Then what is it that you do want to do first thing this morning?

"Guess," she whispered.

His eyes shone as he answered her. "Less talking, more doing."

Those were the last words that were exchanged between them for a long while.

Chapter 19

Sean was utterly convinced that there just were not enough hours in the day. Even if he gave up sleeping altogether and found a way to just run on batteries, he knew he would never be able to get even close to everything accomplished that he needed to. He had loved every moment of the time he'd spent with Orla, but now he had to focus his thoughts on his work.

He had to touch base with Mitch Mallard and see if he'd made any progress in finding Lana's killer—or at least proving who killed her because, in his gut, he already knew who had done away with the young hostess. He hoped Mitch could find the proof to put Wes Westmore away. Her well-to-do fiancé was convinced that he could float through life completely untouched by any consequences for anything he did just because he was such a privileged person.

In addition, Sean still needed to find just what had happened to Humphrey. As the hours passed, they seemed no closer to determining what had become of the psychiatrist. The more research his siblings did, the more questions they came up with. Humphrey had a laundry list of high-profile clients. Right now Cormac was interviewing Assistant District Attorney Emily Hernandez. Sean knew they would keep searching until they found Humphrey—or whoever had harmed him, if that was the case. They wouldn't stop no matter how long it took. They owed the man that much. So far, though, none of them had been able to find a connection between Orla's dead father and the missing Humphrey. They didn't even seem to be business partners. Had Humphrey planted a red herring before he disappeared?

And, of course, he needed to find just where Orla's twin had gone before that woman wound up succeeding in doing something terrible to Orla or someone else.

To that end, he needed to convince his superior, Captain Reeves, that Orla really was innocent of her father's murder. He could tell by the way his captain spoke to him when she called to see how things were going that Reeves was still not fully convinced.

Her doubts would make it harder to prove Orla's innocence.

Leaving his notes on Humphrey's disappearance

for his brothers and Eva to review—he was more than willing to admit that he just might have missed something important—Sean turned his attention toward Orla and clearing that first hurdle, his captain's lingering suspicions.

"Do what you have to do to get ready," he told Orla, walking into the living room after terminating his video conference with his siblings.

Orla looked at him quizzically. That sounded like a very strange thing for him to say. "Are you taking me out?" she asked, amused.

"In a matter of speaking," he told her, closing his computer. "I'm taking you to meet my captain so she can see for herself why I think you're innocent of your father's murder."

"Captain Reeves still has her doubts about the matter?" Orla asked.

Sean thought it best not to pull any punches. "Not as many as before, but yes, I can see it in her eyes, she still does to some extent. I think it would serve our purpose a lot better if you were the one to talk to her and make her realize that you're innocent of any wrongdoing." He smiled at Orla. "After all, the best thing I can say about this matter is that I am not that easily convinced about things. And you managed to convince me."

Her brow furrowed slightly as the meaning of his words sank in. "I didn't try to say anything to convince you that I was innocent. As far as I was concerned, that was just a given from the beginning."

The corners of his mouth turned up ever so slightly. So Orla had never even thought that that was ever up for debate. Sean decided to leave that matter alone. He simply said, "It was the way you didn't say it."

From Orla's expression, it appeared that she didn't know if he was just pulling her leg or was being serious. "You are definitely an enigma, Detective Colton."

"That might be," he granted. "But for the time being, I am your enigma."

Sean looked at Orla's face. How did she feel about being *his* enigma? He couldn't say for sure.

"Let's go," Orla told Sean, gathering her things together. "I'm ready."

Sean was oddly quiet as he drove himself and Orla to the precinct. She had no idea if that was a good sign or not. He still hadn't said a word by the time they arrived at the 130th Precinct and he parked his vehicle outside the building.

She did her best to remain calm as he escorted her inside. This was his superior he was taking her to meet, she thought. Orla had no intentions of allowing her nerves to get the better of her—but it wasn't easy.

Very honestly, she had no idea just who to expect when they walked into the captain's office. It was definitely not the pretty, slightly older, slender blonde who immediately looked up. The next moment, Captain Reeves was on her feet and crossing over to her when she and Sean entered.

The captain's hand was extended toward Orla and at the ready. The smile that followed was slightly delayed but friendly.

"So you did come after all," Captain Reeves acknowledged in mild surprise, her eyes meeting Orla's after briefly nodding toward her detective.

Orla was slightly confused. "I understood that you and Detective Colton had made arrangements about that," she said. "It wouldn't have been very polite of me to avoid this meeting."

She'd almost forgotten the most important detail. "Besides, Detective Colton thought I could do a better job of convincing you that I had nothing to do with my father's murder than he could."

"I'm listening," the captain told her.

Taking a breath, Orla launched into her explanation. "My father and I were both usually too busy working at our separate undertakings to spend time together. But I did love that man dearly," Orla said with feeling. "I always have. Something my twin sister did not," Orla couldn't help adding with more than a little emphasis. "That was her loss."

Captain Reeves took in the information silently. She continued studying Orla without saying a single word. Rising from her seat, the captain quietly circled around Orla, for the moment keeping her thoughts to herself.

Orla kept her eyes forward as the woman made a complete circle around her.

"If you're trying to unnerve me, Captain Reeves,"

she told the older woman, "I have to tell you that compared to my mother, you are, sadly, a mere rank amateur."

"Contrary to what you might think, Ms. Roberts, I am *not* trying to unnerve you," the captain told her. "What I am trying to do is just get a read on you."

The way she said it, it sounded as if Colleen Reeves felt that she'd succeeded.

Orla avoided looking at Sean. She thought the captain might have interpreted that as a sign of weakness. Instead, her eyes never wavered from Reeves's. Orla raised her chin almost pugnaciously.

"And the verdict that you reached?" Orla wanted to know.

Rather than give her an answer, Captain Reeves's eyes shifted toward Sean. The corners of her mouth turned up just a little.

"She's awfully cocky, isn't she?" Reeves asked.

"That was my impression too, after I brushed aside the unhappiness I saw there," Sean told his superior, then explained, "I was with her when she discovered her father's body."

The captain nodded knowingly. "And it is your honest opinion that none of that was orchestrated for your benefit?"

The detective shook his head. "You had to have been there," he told her.

Orla raised her hand as she looked from Reeves to Sean and then back again. "Excuse me, but I'm standing right here, listening to the two of you talking about me," she pointed out.

"Oh yes, I am very aware of that," the captain responded. "Detective Colton brought you in because he felt that you could convince me a lot better of your innocence in this matter than he could."

As she said that, the captain's eyes slowly washed over Orla. And then she smiled at the woman for the first time. Really smiled at her.

"Turns out," Captain Reeves said, "the detective was right. A review of the security tape shows 'you' arriving at your father's building wearing one outfit and then returning in another outfit just before the detective saw you about to go up to your father's apartment. There was no reason for you to change clothes—unless that wasn't you on the tape the first time."

Captain Reeves leaned back for a moment, rocking in her chair and thinking. "Does your twin have any distinguishing marks that could help us tell the two of you apart?" she asked.

Orla sighed and shook her head. "Sadly, we are almost eerily identical—a fact which has contributed to making my life a living hell since I was eight years old. That's why when the time came, I chose a field as far apart from Aimee's as possible."

"How did that work out for you?" Reeves wanted to know.

"Not as well as I would have wanted. Especially when we wound up going to the same college. At the time, I really thought that meant we were getting closer." Orla laughed under her breath, shaking her head. There was absolutely no humor in the sound. "You would have thought after all those years, I would have known better."

"How so?" the captain asked. Out of the corner of her eye, Reeves saw her detective shaking his head at her, but it was too late for her to retreat.

"Aimee really enjoyed showing me up. Not only that, but she also enjoyed belittling me and making me pay, big-time," Orla said.

"Making you pay?" the captain echoed. "Making you pay for what?"

"As near as I can figure, making me pay for looking just like her. What that meant was that in her mind, she wasn't the unique creature she thought she was. That was ultimately, I'm betting, also the reason why Aimee wound up killing our father."

Reeves looked from Sean to Orla. "Enlighten me again about that," she requested, as if she was at a loss as to the cause and consequences.

"Because I existed, our father did not leave his money entirely to her. In the last will that he filed, our father specified that the money be split three ways, dividing it equally between Aimee, our mother and myself. There were a number of charities thrown into the mix as well.

"I found out that my mother was out of town when my father was killed, but not Aimee. I have a feeling that when Aimee went to see our father in his apartment, she couldn't get him to agree to her plans. Aimee was known to have a quick, sharp temper and I have no doubt that she lost it. He probably said something to Aimee that caused her to fly into a rage. Possibly something to the effect that he wouldn't be doing her a service if he gave her all the money."

Orla grew misty, thinking back. "My father was a firm believer that money meant more if you had to earn at least some of it." She stared at the wall, tears gathering in her eyes as she envisioned what had transpired. "My guess is that Aimee snapped at him and probably just lost it. Sadly, the rest turned out to be predictable history. But because the doorman or someone else wound up surprising her, Aimee didn't get a chance to clean up after herself."

The captain exchanged looks with her detective, then looked back at her. "Sounds pretty believable to me," Captain Reeves told Orla.

Sean's smile widened. He looked rather satisfied with himself for having made the decision to bring his captain and Orla together.

"So you're killing any arrest warrants that might be on the books for Orla?" he asked.

"I rewatched the security footage twice. Aimee might have the same face as her sister, but she dresses entirely differently and her very manner fairly shouts of entitlement. Unless something comes up to make me see things in a different light—which I highly doubt is going to happen at this point—consider those arrest warrants issued for Ms. Orla Roberts put to bed," she told him. "Now go, find out just where Aimee Roberts went to—and bring her in."

Orla rose from the chair in front of the captain's desk. She didn't wait for Sean to say anything. "I fully intend to, Captain."

If she was surprised that Orla responded instead of Sean, she didn't say anything. Orla felt a ton of bricks lift from her shoulders. It was as if she had been given a brand-new lease on life.

She gave Sean a smile and he fell into step beside her as they walked out of the captain's office.

Chapter 20

Sean had no sooner gotten into his vehicle after opening the door and holding it for Orla than his cell phone rang.

"Maybe your captain changed her mind," was Orla's first guess.

Sean took out his phone and glanced at the screen. "It's not the captain," he told her.

"Hi, Eva. What's up?" Sean asked, leaving his key in the ignition. For now, he didn't bother to turn it.

"You want to say thank you now, or later?" Eva asked her older brother.

"Okay, I'll bite. What is it that I'm thanking you for?" He glanced in Orla's direction. His gut feeling told him that this had something to do with her.

"As you probably know, I attached myself to the CSI team and gave Rockwell Roberts's apartment a more thorough once-over, looking for fingerprints. You might remember that we weren't able to find any the first time around."

She was stretching this out, Sean thought. He decided to indulge her—for now. "Go on," he urged.

"Well, they were right about there not being any of Aimee's prints *anywhere*," Eva emphasized.

"But?" he asked expectantly, waiting for her to get to the punch line. He could see Orla shifting in her seat, leaning in closer. "Get to the point, Eva, while we're all still young."

"But I found a couple of fingerprints at the scene. Clean ones and they belonged to Orla's twin."

Sean instantly straightened up. Despite her eagerness in solving crimes, Eva didn't allow that eagerness to have her make any mistakes.

"You found Aimee's fingerprints at the scene?" he asked, wanting to be sure of what his sister was saying.

"Yes I did," she replied proudly. "Two very clear ones."

"Tell the captain," Sean instructed.

"I will, I just thought I should tell you first since up until now, things were looking pretty bleak," his sister explained.

"You did good, kid. Now go tell Captain Reeves," he repeated, "since she's in charge of the investigation."

"Will do," Eva promised, her satisfaction evident in her voice.

"This is good," Orla said as Sean terminated the call.

"I didn't realize that you had a gift for understatement—but yes, this is good. Now the captain is focusing on your sister for both her prison escape as well as your father's murder.

"*Now* can we set a trap for Aimee so we can bring her in?" she asked Sean as he started up his car.

There was something in her voice that triggered him. "You have an idea?"

Orla smiled and nodded. "I have an idea."

He didn't trust her. She could be reckless. "On a scale of one to ten, just how dangerous is it?" Sean wanted to know.

"How dangerous it is isn't the point," she told him.

That was what he was afraid of. "It's not the point only if you happen to be a bulletproof superhero," he pointed out.

"Don't worry," Orla assured him. "I can handle myself."

"I'm sure your father thought the same thing," Sean said solemnly.

Orla's eyes flashed. "That's a low blow," she accused.

"It's an accurate one," Sean countered. Temporarily pulling his car over to the curb, he stopped driving. "The only thing that matters here is that nothing happens to you. Everything else, including proving your sister's guilt, is secondary. Have I made myself clear?" Sean demanded.

Orla sighed, sounding irritated as she stared straight ahead. "You have to say that," she insisted. "You're a police detective."

"No, I don't *have* to say anything," Sean pointed out tersely. "What I *need* to do is emphasize the truth. Now tell me this plan of yours and I'll tell you just how doable it is."

"I am going to go back to my father's place to spend the night. With any luck—" She never got the chance to finish her statement.

"Not without me you don't," Sean cut in. "Aimee is not going to believe that you've suddenly turned reckless. Or stupid."

"It's not a matter of being reckless—or stupid," she told him. "It's a matter of thumbing my nose at her."

"And that's not reckless?" he questioned in disbelief.

"No, it's a matter of my not viewing her as an imminent threat. She knows that she doesn't have me shaking in my shoes, she never has."

"I think that might be part of what drives her," Sean admitted. "She *wants* you to be afraid of her. From what you've told me, she has been competing against you all of her life. Her goal is to be able to come out on top and you haven't allowed her to do that. That's probably why she set her sights on your boyfriend and stole him from you."

Orla inclined her head as if considering what he'd said.

"You're right," she finally allowed.

He'd expected more of a fight than that. "By the way," he began.

The tone of his voice must have caught her attention. "Yes?"

"What did you see in him?"

She shrugged carelessly. "At the time I thought he was cute and sexy. Everyone is entitled to one stupid mistake."

"Maybe the average person is," Sean allowed. "But not you."

"Are you saying that I'm above average?" She smiled.

"I'm saying that I think you're smarter than that," he told her.

"Well, smarter or not, the best way to draw her out is to be out there in plain sight. I'm counting on the fact that her hatred of me is greater than her ability to reason things out."

"Maybe," Sean said. "But she's driven by her hatred of you and that just might outweigh everything else. I'm not about to have you out there on your own where she can get at you. Whatever else your twin might be, she is not stupid."

"No, but her hatred of me just might be blinding," Orla pointed out.

"Is there any logical reason why she hates you as much as she does" he wanted to know. From everything Orla had told him, it just didn't make any sense. He and his siblings could be at odds with one another at times, but when push came to shove, they were always in each other's corners.

"I gave up trying to understand why Aimee hates me as much as she does," Orla said honestly. "For whatever reason is driving her, it just seems to be a given. As far back as I can remember, she acted out every single time my father treated me with respect, or kindness, or acknowledged something I had done.

"Don't get me wrong. It wasn't all that often, but even once was too much in her eyes. And," Orla continued, "nothing I ever did for her was ever good enough, so eventually, I just gave up trying. I kept my distance from her whenever I could." Orla shook her head. "I foolishly believed my father and I were safe when she and Joe were sent to prison." She frowned deeply. "Shows you how naive I was," Orla murmured.

She looked off into the distance, as if she was reliving every second of what had transpired. Orla lowered her voice. It was filled with emotion. "Aimee really crossed the line when she took her anger out on our father and killed him."

Visibly trying to subdue her anger, she looked up

at him. "I honestly believe that she is never going to be happy until she kills me too. And most likely," Orla whispered, "not even then."

"This plan of yours," Sean began, deciding that whatever it was, he wanted to talk her out of it.

Orla shook her head, stopping Sean before he could go any further. "I have to do it, Sean. I have to be the bait so that you can capture her. It's the only chance I'm going to have for a normal life," she told him. "I know I'll never have it if she's out there somewhere, walking around. I'll be forced to spend the rest of my life looking over my shoulder, waiting for Aimee to pop out of the shadows to kill me. Trust me, I know her well enough to tell you that she can easily do that without even blinking an eye."

"I know exactly what you're saying, but damn it, I don't like...I don't like any of it," he said vehemently.

"The alternative is for me to keep on running for the rest of my life and even then there is no guarantee that I'll ever be safe. My only choice is to have her come after me where I—where *we*," she amended, "can have at least some control over the outcome."

"All right," Sean agreed reluctantly. "I understand your reasoning in this. I don't like it," he deliberately emphasized, "but I can understand it." He blew out a deep breath as he resumed driving back to his apartment with her. "Exactly what is your plan?" he finally asked her.

"I plan to go back to my own place tomorrow," she explained, "and live there when I'm not out working."

"Working," he echoed. "So you're going back to business as usual?" The question echoed of skepticism.

"I'm treating the situation the way anyone would. After the services are held and a burial of sorts occurs," she said, talking in general, "life slowly goes back to normal."

"We have a completely different definition of *normal*," he told her. The wheels in his head began turning. "Since you won over the captain, I'm going to use that to have her give me as many people as she can spare to help me guard you."

"Well, unless Aimee and Joe have managed to put together a crew—and that's highly doubtful—there's only going to be the two of them. I don't need a whole bunch of people surrounding me and providing me with protection. *Really*," she emphasized.

"You know what they used to call a gun in the Old West?" he asked her. Before she could answer, he did. "They referred to it as 'the great equalizer.'" He looked at her. "There's a reason for that. Want to guess what that was?"

"I don't have to guess. I know. I don't want Aimee scared off," she insisted. "Or this will never end."

"Trust me, my people know how to be invisible. Your sister, unless she has some sort of X-ray vision and possibly even superpowers, will never see them. This may not seem like it to you," he pointed out, "but this is actually a compromise. It's the only one you're going to get out of me, so I suggest you take it. Otherwise, I'm going to wrap you up in plastic and put you in a closet for the foreseeable future. Have I made myself clear?"

"You're going to force me to go along with this?" she asked, making no effort to hide her surprise.

"With every fiber of my being, if it ensures that you go along with this and, more importantly, that I manage to keep you alive."

She sighed. "So I have no choice when it comes to this?" she persisted.

"Nope," he answered complacently. It was funny how much he'd agonized over this and now that he had made up his mind to carry it out, the whole process was painless and exceedingly easily handled. "This is the only compromise I'm about to offer."

She sighed again. "I guess I don't have a choice if I want this to get off the ground in any fashion."

"You do not," he assured her. "Personally, this method has its merits."

"That's not the way I see it," she told him.

"Yeah, I figured you would say that," he said. "I'll take you to your place tomorrow, but for tonight, we're going to pretend that none of this exists. And that we're just two very hot, oversexed people who are extremely determined to enjoy one another and have as many moments as they are able to muster between them."

"Isn't that rather a simplistic way to view this?" Orla asked him.

"Simplistic is exactly what I was shooting for."

He winked. "You don't have a problem with that, do you?"

Orla couldn't help smiling. "Who me? Not at all. I do have a problem with going to bed so early, but I can probably see my way clear in that too." Humor glinted in her eyes.

Sean's smile reached his eyes and lingered there. "I had a feeling that you might be able to manage that," he told her. "We can pack up your things in the morning."

She threaded her fingers through his hair.

"Works for me," she whispered against his mouth.

Chapter 21

Orla really hadn't slept all that much in two days now. Going on three, actually.

That was how long she'd been waiting for Aimee to make an appearance in her apartment. In her life for that matter.

Doing her best not to look obvious about it, Orla kept looking around for her sister and just possibly Joe as well to pop up in her life. To come grab her and drag her away.

So far, nothing.

Was that just a coincidence, or was that by design? Orla had no idea, although she did harbor her suspicions.

What really amazed her was just how much she

missed Sean. He'd been in her life an incredibly short amount of time, yet she couldn't imagine life without him.

Perforce, he had to keep his distance from her while she went about life the way she had before any of this had gone into high gear.

"When this thing ends," she whispered to herself, "you are going to wind up being a basket case."

"Did you say something?" the curvy blonde she'd recently taken on as a student asked her. They were working out in a private gym and the woman, Robin Hines, frowned a little as she appeared to be replaying what her instructor had just said.

Orla shook her head. "No, just going over what we need to cover next time." She smiled at her student. "You're coming along very nicely," she told Robin. "Making a lot of progress," she added.

Her latest student beamed, pleased with the compliment.

"I'll see you tomorrow, same time?" Robin asked, assuming that the answer was yes.

"Yes," Orla answered. *Unless Aimee has other plans.* She knew it would take very little for her sister to kidnap her and take her place—except for the glaring fact that Aimee hadn't a clue how to do any of these moves, she thought. If she even attempted to conduct a class, that would be a dead giveaway.

The cell phone that was all but hermetically glued to her side rang. Orla raised her hand, cutting her student short.

"If you'll excuse me, I have to take this. I'll see you tomorrow," she told Robin with a false cheerfulness she didn't feel.

Robin nodded and left the small gym. Orla put the phone against her ear. Sean's deep voice filled her head. A sense of happiness flooded all through her. "So, how's it going?" he asked.

"The same as when you asked the last time. Sean, you have to stop worrying," she told him, knowing full well that she would be worried about him if their places were reversed.

"Sorry, it comes with the badge."

"Sean, I really appreciate your concern, but you're going to make yourself crazy," Orla said.

"I'll keep that in mind," he answered. "So, by my reckoning, you've just seen your last student of the day. That means you're going home now, right?"

Like he didn't know, she thought. "That was the plan, yes."

Sean got down to the reason he'd called. "How about we skip going to your place and I'll just take you to mine for the night. We can resume this cat-and-mouse game again tomorrow," he suggested.

He was making this really hard for her. She wanted nothing more than to be with him, but that wouldn't solve the problem that was hovering over her.

"That was *not* the plan," she reminded the detective. "Sean, I don't like this any more than you do—"

"Okay, go home. I'll check on you later."

She smiled to herself. Funny how such a simple

phrase could warm her heart so much. The man had completely changed her in such a short amount of time, Orla couldn't help thinking.

On her way out of the gym she passed a couple of faces that looked vaguely familiar to her, but that could very well just be her imagination.

More than anything, she wished that this whole thing was over. But knowing how Aimee operated, this so-called adventure could very well drag on forever.

And then, when she least expected it, she thought with a sinking feeling, Aimee and Joe would pounce.

She needed to keep a clear head. Otherwise, she was going to drive herself crazy and then she wouldn't be any good to herself—or to anyone else.

Orla drove herself to her father's apartment. Now that he was gone, the place was hers. She knew that fact irritated Aimee beyond words, which was the reason she was staying in it. If Aimee was going to try and execute vengeance on her, she knew it would be here. Staying in the apartment where her father had been brutally murdered wasn't easy, but Orla knew it was necessary if she wanted to lure her twin into the trap.

She just hoped that it would be soon before she turned into a zombie up all night.

Walking into the luxury building, Orla greeted Harold. This doorman was a stand-in for Edgar, the one who had been on duty when her father was killed. Management was not sure whether or not to let the man off the hook for being oblivious to Aimee doing away with her father.

They didn't know Aimee the way she did, Orla thought, her heart hardening.

It was the surprised look on Harold's face that alerted her. She'd passed him before, both coming and going, and he hadn't looked surprised at that time. But he did now. That could only mean one thing as far as she was concerned. That he'd already seen her coming in this afternoon.

Seen her coming in and not going back out again. Yet here she was, coming in for a second time.

Aimee had to be here, Orla thought. Either that, or she was getting way too uptight about the situation, she thought.

She took a deep breath, telling herself that she had to stop making herself crazy like this. If she continued on this path, she would be playing right into Aimee's hands and doing half of her twin's work for her.

Concentrating on placing one foot in front of the other, Orla let herself into the spacious apartment. Every single one of her senses was on the alert as she slowly scanned the area. But the apartment was quiet, almost eerily so.

Maybe Aimee would succeed in making her crazy without even trying or lifting a finger.

She took another long, deep breath, attempting to calm herself. What would be would be. Worrying about it ahead of time was not going to accomplish anything for her.

She knew that Sean was waiting for her to check in. Orla decided to do that before she turned her attention to something mundane like making dinner.

Sean was the first number on her cell phone, but she barely had a chance to press number one before she heard an all too familiar voice behind her. "Still slaving away at those piddling jobs of yours, Orla? I am really ashamed that you and I share the same face, making people think that we are one and the same person," Aimee said, sending a cold chill down her spine.

With a covert movement, Orla slipped her phone into her pocket, making sure to leave the cell phone on. She fervently hoped that Sean would just listen and not say anything to alert Aimee that he was there.

Orla turned slowly around. Aimee actually looked cheerful. "How did you manage to get in here, Aimee?"

"The same way I did the last time," she told her twin. "I approached the doorman." Aimee put on an exceedingly sad face as she blinked her eyelashes. "'I lost my keys. Could you let me in?' And of course he did because the help here all know who I am," she said with a nasty laugh. And then her expression turned ugly. "I'm the big-time Realtor's daughter. Seems that they can't distinguish between the two of us. Well, that's not going to be a problem much longer."

"And why is that?" Orla asked, her eyes pinning her twin down. She knew perfectly well what Aimee's answer was going to be. She was hoping that pride would cause Aimee to make a mistake.

Her expression grew darker as she drew closer to Orla. "Because there's only going to *be* one of us very soon. Maybe even by the end of the night," she said confidently.

"You sound very sure of yourself." Orla's eyes narrowed. "Are you going to have that spineless wimp of a lover of yours shoot me?" she wanted to know.

Aimee tossed her head, insulted. "What's the matter, you think you're so tough, you think I can't take you without his help?" Her tone had turned utterly vicious.

Orla looked at her twin coldly. She saw no sign of Joe yet. Her best bet, if he did turn up, was to throw Joe off. In her opinion, he'd always been a coward.

She was carefully watching every move Aimee made. "Actually, I don't think the two of you are capable of taking me on unless one of you is holding me down while the other is shooting me," she told her sister. "A gun is your weapon of choice, isn't it?"

The smile that rose on Aimee's lips was blood-curdlingly nasty. It was obvious that she liked the idea. "Shooting you," she repeated with relish. "You think so?"

Orla was convinced that getting Aimee riled up

was the best way to ensure that her twin would slip up and be unable to get the better of her.

"I *know* so," she told Aimee with unerring confidence.

Aimee shrieked her indignation, her hands outstretched as she lunged forward, ready to dig her nails into Orla's flesh.

Orla moved deftly aside, then grabbed Aimee's arms, throwing her twin to the ground.

It was no contest. Orla had a black belt in martial arts while Aimee only knew how to party. The match between them was short-lived, especially since Orla was aware that her life was on the line. This wasn't a match she had any intention of losing.

Not legitimately at any rate.

But then she saw Joe come barreling in through the opened door, his gun raised and ready to fire.

"You're cheating again!" Orla accused.

She ducked just in time to miss being hit, then dove for Joe's legs, throwing him completely off-balance. He landed against Aimee.

"Put the damn gun away, Joe!" Orla shouted at him.

"I'd listen to the lady if I were you," Sean said from behind him.

Sean must have expected Joe to drop the weapon. Instead, infuriated, he swirled around and aimed the handgun at Sean, firing it and hitting the detective in the shoulder. Sean returned the favor.

Joe squealed like a pig, grabbing his chest. Blood

oozed from between his fingers. Aimee cursed as she shook her head. She grabbed Joe's hand and took charge, quickly pulling him out of the apartment.

Orla's heart dropped. She rocked back on her heels, pushing aside Sean's jacket and shirt.

"How bad is it?" she wanted to know, closely examining the area.

"I'll live," he told her, although he grimaced as she checked out his wound. He attempted to get up but there was no way Orla was going to let him.

"Your chances will improve greatly if we have that wound cleaned out and bandaged," Orla informed him.

"We don't have time to go to the hospital to get this taken care of," Sean insisted.

She was already on her way to the bathroom. "Who said anything about a hospital? One of the things I did when I began teaching self-defense classes was learn how to take care of the injuries that were certain to crop up."

Sean looked at her rather dubiously. "Are you any good?"

"Well, we are about to find out," she answered. "Come in here and sit down," she instructed, nodding toward the bathroom. "I realize that I've giving up any chance of capturing my rotten twin, but I'm not about to have you bleed out just to give Aimee what she has coming to her. Saving you takes precedence over not having to look over my shoulder for the rest of my life."

He gritted his teeth while she carefully probed his shoulder, finally locating the bullet. "You patch me up fast enough and you might be able to do both."

She raised her eyes to his face as she went on working. "I think that wound has just made you delirious." Orla carefully pulled the bullet out of his shoulder.

She could have sworn that she felt it as much as he did.

"Not really," Sean denied, wincing. "I spotted your sister's car just before I ran into the building. I planted a tracker just beneath the bumper in case she and that boyfriend of hers took off. I don't intend to lose track of that pair twice," he told her.

Orla cleaned out the wound as best she could, bandaging him up after having extracted the bullet. Finished, she carefully applied tape to keep the bandages in place.

"Done," she declared. "That should hold—unless you suddenly decide to go scuba diving," she added with a smile.

She couldn't help thinking that had been much too close for comfort.

Sean reached for what was left of his shirt. "Not on my list of things to do. Getting your twin and her slimeball of a boyfriend, though, definitely is," Sean told her.

She saw the pain registering in his eyes and delicately helped Sean on with his shirt and then his jacket. She knew that Sean meant exactly what he said.

"Then I suggest we get to it. But if you start to look exhausted," she warned him, "I'm planning on making you go to the ER."

He looked at her, laughing under his breath. "You really are bossy, aren't you?"

Getting her purse, Orla didn't bother even trying to deny it. "You have no idea, Detective. You have *no* idea."

Chapter 22

"Are you getting a signal?" Orla asked as she got into Sean's car. She had wanted to be the one behind the wheel, but he'd insisted he was fine and they really didn't have time to argue about it.

"It's faint," he told her, "But I am definitely getting a signal." Sean looked at his dashboard. "It looks like she's heading upstate." Sean turned toward Orla as he carefully wove his way through the city streets.

To his recollection, morning, noon or night, there never seemed to be a time when traffic wasn't clogging the streets. "What's upstate?" he asked her.

She shook her head. "Nothing that I'm aware of. At least nothing that means anything to either one of us. Aimee always liked haunting the big cities, the bigger the better, especially when it came to exclusive shopping. Aimee is definitely not a country girl. I think right now she's just trying to escape in order to be able to come back and fight another day. This time killing me."

She said it so matter-of-factly, it really bothered Sean. "Well, she's not going to," he told her with finality.

"I think that the driving force in her life right now is getting rid of me. Once she accomplishes that, who knows," she said with a shrug.

"Well, she damn well isn't going to accomplish that. Not now, not ever," Sean informed her with feeling, adding, "Not if I have anything to say about it."

"Aimee likes to immerse herself in playing psychological warfare," she said. "I found that the only way to deal with all that is just to shrug it off. Anything else and I will be playing this sick game on her terms and that way only lies failure."

Sean nodded. "There has to be a way to get her locked up for good," he told her with conviction. Aimee didn't deserve to breathe the same air as Orla, he couldn't help thinking.

Orla smiled wistfully as she nodded. "First we have to catch her, then we can focus on doing that."

He kept glancing at the signal that was registering on his dashboard, moving northward. The signal represented Aimee and her boyfriend.

"Right," he agreed. "First things first."

* * *

The chase continued through the city all the way up the coast along the Hudson River.

Sean was more than just a decent driver, he was an exceedingly good driver. All he needed to do was just acquaint himself with an area once and he could find his way around. But even so, he didn't trust anything to be as straightforward as it appeared.

At least, not this straightforward, he thought. Eager to overtake the fleeing duo, he still forced himself to slow down, at least to a degree.

"You're slowing down," Orla noticed, questioning what he was up to.

Sean nodded. He supposed she wanted him to give her a reason. He obliged. "I don't want to pass them, and I don't want to take a chance on running into them unless I'm fully prepared for that to happen." And right now, his strength hadn't fully returned. He was still fighting off the effects of the gunshot wound.

Because he was being so careful, careful and alert, neither he nor Orla were prepared to all but run into Joe's vehicle suddenly.

The road was exceedingly narrow at that point and maneuvering for space was especially tricky.

Too tricky it turned out.

It felt as if they were actually fighting for space on the winding road. He could have sworn that there was enough space available for both vehicles but a sudden move on Joe's part negated that.

The very next moment, the car Joe and Aimee were in dipped and then suddenly went off the cliff.

It all happened so suddenly, Sean couldn't decide if the car had gone over the side by accident—or if it had happened on purpose.

He was barely able to keep his own vehicle from plunging over the side. Holding on to the wheel he struggled to make the car's back wheels halt what seemed like their eminent plunge over the side of the winding road.

A small shriek managed to escape Orla's lips despite the fact that she had them pressed together.

The road ahead of them began to widen. Sean's heart pounded madly as he realized how close to dying they had come.

"Are you all right?" he asked Orla.

She was struggling to regulate her breathing. "A lot better now than I would have been if there'd been a different outcome to this little road trip we just took," she told him.

Orla stuck her head out the window, taking in the full scene.

She glanced toward Sean. "Do you think there's any chance that their car didn't crash at the bottom of the road?"

He laughed dryly, really relieved that they were breathing. "About as much chance as the car suddenly sprouting wings and flying."

"So in other words, no," Orla guessed.

"In any words, no," Sean told her.

Leaning back against her seat, Orla took in several deep breaths.

After a minute had passed, she told him, "Drive down the road."

He knew what she was asking him to do—and why. "Are you sure you're ready to take this all in?" he asked. "You know that the results aren't going to be pretty."

"I'm not an idiot," she muttered. "I know that."

"No one is accusing you of being an idiot, Orla," he said. "I just don't want to be responsible for aiding and abetting your nightmares. If that car did hit bottom—and I figure that it had to—it and the passengers in it are going to be literally in pieces…or in flames. Are you ready to see that?"

"I'm ready for this nightmare that I've been living for the last thirty-five years to finally be over," she told him.

"Well, I've got to say that that's a very healthy way to look at it."

"That is the *only* way to look at it," she replied.

He nodded but didn't attempt to start up the vehicle just yet. "I'm still going to have to call this into the department before we drive down and take a look for ourselves."

"Tell me whatever you need me to do," she said with a wave of her hand. "I will do whatever you need me to do in order to help out."

He nodded. "I appreciate that." He didn't want

any blame falling on her, and he was grateful that for once she didn't argue with him.

Fighting the urge to call in his brothers, Sean dutifully filed an official report with Captain Reeves. It would all be on record and hopefully any questions about the matter would be handled.

Both Orla and Sean were surprised to see Captain Reeves come to the scene of the accident herself.

Her expression was grim when she got out of her vehicle. "So just what happened?" Reeves wanted to know.

Sean was the one who gave his superior a report. "We put a tracker on Aimee Roberts's vehicle and we were following her," the detective told his superior.

"But the choice to drive off the cliff was all hers," Orla quickly told Captain Reeves. "I know for certain that Aimee didn't want to be hauled off to prison a second time, especially if she believed that I was the one responsible for her capture."

Colleen Reeves looked at Orla, debating whether or not to take her at her word. From everything she had learned about the other woman, Orla's explanation sounded plausible. "You really think so?" she finally asked.

"Oh, I know so. She has—*had*," Orla corrected, "been competing against me for what seems like her entire life. No matter what was at stake, Aimee treated it as if it was a vital competition between us. She couldn't stand the idea of my being better at *anything* than she was. Because of her poisonous attitude, I did my best to keep away from her whenever I could."

The captain nodded. "Sounds like the two of you had an interesting dynamic," she concluded.

"That wouldn't be the word I would use, but yes, that would be one word for it," Orla reluctantly agreed.

Reeves looked at Sean's torn shirt and jacket. "Why don't you go to the ER and have that seen to?" she suggested.

"Orla already took care of it for me," Sean told his superior.

"Do as the captain says. I'll drive," she stressed.

Sean's mouth curved. "Then I'll really need the ER," he quipped.

"Very funny," Orla responded, shutting him down.

Just then Aimee and Joe's bodies were brought over on two gurneys and placed into the wagon. Orla's attention temporarily shifted.

It is over, she thought. *Finally over.*

For just a moment, she felt deep regret over the way this had ended. Once upon a time, she believed she and Aimee could have been friends, or at the very least not the enemies that Aimee was convinced that they were.

Goodbye, Aimee. Orla watched the ambulance doors close on the mangled bodies that had been loaded onto the transport. *You have no idea what you missed out on*, she silently told her sister.

Turning toward Sean, she pasted a smile on her lips and said, "All right, let's have someone official look at those bandages and tell me whether or not I did a credible job placing them on you."

"Hey, I'm satisfied," he told her.

"That's all very nice, but I'm not. Move it, Detective. I'm taking you to the hospital to be officially checked out. If they say your wound isn't infected, *then* I'm happy." Her eyes met his. "There is no middle ground, Colton," she informed him. "You have to do what I say."

He sighed, apparently understanding there was no winning this argument. "All right," he agreed grudgingly. "But I'm not happy about this."

"Happiness is not a requirement here," she said. "All you need to do is just go along with being seen in the ER."

They waited at the hospital ER a lot longer than he was happy about. Several times he tried to convince her just to pick up and leave the hospital with him, but she refused to.

"You need to see one of the doctors and that's the end of the discussion," she insisted.

He didn't like being ordered around, but he knew her heart was in the right place, so he remained where he was, doing his best to tap into what was left of his patience.

Eventually, he knew, his patience would be rewarded and besides, this would give him something to hold over her head, he thought.

He just hoped that it would be sooner than later.

Chapter 23

Wilson Jamison, the ER doctor who was on duty when Sean came in, carefully examined the wound that was beneath the bandage. He solemnly nodded his head.

"Whoever did this did a really good job," the physician informed Sean. "Quite honestly, there's really nothing for me to do except to rebandage the wound, give you some antibiotics plus a few painkillers and tell you not to get the wound wet. Have your own doctor look at it again in a week. It should be on its way to being healed by then," he told Sean.

Sean exchanged looks with Orla and smiled. "Good to know, Doctor," he said. He would have told the physician that the person who'd taken care of his wound was sitting in the exam room with him, but he had a feeling that Orla wouldn't have welcomed having any sort of attention focused on her.

They were back on the road and on the way to his home in less than an hour after that.

"Good thing you were there," Sean told her.

"I don't know about that," she contradicted. "If I wasn't there, you wouldn't have gotten shot trying to save me."

Sean blew out a breath as he pulled his vehicle into underground parking. "Can you please just learn to take a compliment?" he asked.

"I will—when it's deserved," she answered.

"Well, I for one think it's deserved," he said. "As a matter of fact, I happen to think that we're pretty perfect together."

Sean was aware that he was going out on a limb here. Very honestly, he didn't ordinarily say things like that. Even though he had been engaged twice, he had *never* said anything like that to either one of the two women he'd been engaged to. But that was because he had never felt anything for either one of those women that even remotely came close to what he was feeling right now for Orla.

"'*Together*' is a very loaded word," Orla told him quietly. "At this point in my life, I realize that I'm a lone wolf and most likely, always will be."

"We've gone through a lot," he said. "Things will look a lot better in the morning. I think we could both do with a good night's sleep."

She nodded. "In our own beds," she said, planning on going to her apartment once she retrieved her car. Getting out of his car, she told him, "I'll see you in the morning—or soon."

He'd gotten out of his car and was about to walk her to where she had left hers parked at her father's building, but then had second thoughts about that. It was obvious that she wanted to be alone. "Whatever you want," he told her.

This was really ironic, he couldn't help thinking. The one woman he found himself attracted to and wanting was actually backing off from him.

Who would have thought it?

But he had a feeling that the more he pushed, the more she *would* back away from him. He needed to apply the patience he usually employed in following up on his cases and use it here—if he wanted to have a prayer of winning her over.

Just before she got into her car, she turned toward him and said, "Don't forget to take care of that wound."

"I will," he replied.

She was doing the right thing, Orla told herself. She didn't want to get caught up in a relationship and risk getting slammed with the sort of pain that being involved with someone brought with it. Her father's death had traumatized her and in its own way, Aimee sailing over the side of the cliff had done the same.

It was better not to have any relationships at all than to leave herself open to this sort of pain.

The thought haunted her for close to two weeks. It was there when she first opened her eyes in the morning and there when she finally closed them at night to get a tiny bit of sleep.

She could feel it constantly eating away at her, taking chunks out of her when she was least prepared for it.

What in heaven's name was going on with her, she silently demanded for the umpteenth time. Rather than having this separation from Sean calm her down, it only seemed to be making things worse.

Being a lone wolf was for the birds, she told herself. She realized that when she had been around Sean, working with him, was the only time that she truly felt whole.

Moreover, being around Sean succeeded in making her happy.

And being happy, she realized, actually brightened her life.

She was not used to that, she realized, and at first she held that "condition" highly suspect. This happiness, she told herself, was baseless—but feeling this way was exquisite and, even if it lasted just a little while, it was better than moving through life numb and without it.

She needed to change things up. Even if it all wound up exploding in her face, in the end it would be worth it. A little bit of happiness was better than a life of numbing tranquility.

Several of the clues he'd followed had led him nowhere. Sean and his siblings were no closer to locating Humphrey Kelly than they had been at the start of this, but none of them were about to give up.

Besides, he needed to keep busy because if he was busy, he wouldn't think about the gut-wrenching pain he felt when his thoughts turned toward Orla being out of his life.

When he heard the knock on the door that evening, his first thought was to grab his weapon. He was not the type to take chances.

Picking his gun up, Sean crossed to the door. He flipped the lock and then cautiously opened it. When he saw Orla standing there, his first thought was that he was hallucinating.

But she didn't fade away. She remained right where she was.

"Something wrong?" he asked, thinking that there had to be to bring her here.

"Well, you're not inviting me in," she told him, answering his question.

"Sorry," he apologized, opening the door all the way. "Come on in," he invited. Sean shut the door behind her. Securing the lock, he turned to look at her. "Has there been some sort of a new development?" He refused to allow himself to believe that she had voluntarily come back into his life.

It couldn't be so simple. Something else had to be going on.

"You might say that," Orla replied haltingly.

"Oh?" That was a loaded phrase, he thought. "What else might I say?" he asked, picking up on her phraseology.

"That I've changed," she said.

He was not going to allow himself to get excited. The letdown would be too much to bear. So he asked cautiously, "How have you changed?"

He was going to make her pay for what she'd put him through, Orla thought. Well, she knew that it was only fair.

Recalling the way she had worded her exit line, she told him, "I've decided that my 'lone wolf' days are over and behind me now." He wasn't saying anything, she noticed. She had this coming to her and she couldn't blame him, but she intended to do whatever she had to do to make him forgive her. Her walking away from him, from them, had been the biggest mistake she'd ever made. In trying to protect herself, she had almost ruined the glimmer of happiness that had unexpectedly materialized in her life.

"When I was here last time, you mentioned something about a life partner role." Her voice trailed off for a moment.

"What about it?" he asked innocently.

Orla took in a deep breath, trying to calm herself.

"Well, if it's still on the table—and you were serious about it—I think I'd like to take it on."

For a moment, he said nothing. "You'd 'like to'?" he asked, looking at her closely.

She closed her eyes for a moment. This was harder to get out than she had initially imagined. But she had to.

"All right," she told him, "I *want* to take it on."

Sean smiled at her, really smiled, his face lighting up.

Drawing Orla into his arms, he kissed her, hard and with feeling. "You made me very happy, coming here," he said. "This means I won't have to kidnap you."

Relief washed all through her. "Then we're all right?" she asked Sean.

"We're more than all right," he told her before he took her back into his arms and showed her just how "all right" they really were.

Sean went on showing her for quite some time.

Fortunately, he had finished "showing" her just when the doorbell rang.

He sighed. "Maybe they'll go away," he said to Orla.

"And maybe whoever it is will continue ringing the doorbell. You'd better go answer it," she said, quickly getting dressed.

Leaving off his shirt, Sean padded over to the door, barefoot but taking his weapon with him just in case.

When he opened the door, Cormac did a double

take at the gun in Sean's hand. "Well hello to you, too." He nodded at Orla as the others entered behind him. "Something we should know about?" he asked, looking from Sean to Orla.

"You look happy," Eva commented.

Laying the weapon aside, Sean drew Orla into his arms. "We are happy," he confirmed as Orla nodded in agreement.

"Looks like you finally found a commitment that works for you. Too bad it wouldn't for me," Cormac said philosophically.

"Not that I don't like your company," Sean said to his siblings, "but why are you here?"

"We came to tell you that we're not going to give up looking for Uncle Humphrey until we find him," Eva volunteered.

"And now you two," Liam said, putting an arm around Eva and Cormac as he directed them back through the door, "can go back to doing whatever it was that you were doing," he said cheerfully, closing the door behind all three of them.

Sean grinned at Orla. "Sounds good to me," he whispered into her ear.

Neither needed any more encouragement than that.

* * * * *

*Don't miss the next installment of
the Coltons of New York*

Protecting Colton's Baby
by Tara Taylor Quinn

*Out in February 2023 from
Harlequin Romantic Suspense!*

*For a sneak peek at the next
Coltons of New York story*

Protecting Colton's Baby,
by Tara Taylor Quinn

turn the page...

Chapter 1

A forty-three-year-old woman did not belong in front of the shelf of home pregnancy tests.

She just didn't.

Assistant District Attorney Emily Hernandez had made a solid career out of getting facts right.

Statistics said that hormones to fight bone density were in her future, not supplements that would stabilize and facilitate a healthy fetus.

When a young mother with a toddler in tow entered the aisle, Emily had to step forward to let her pass. The plump-legged little girl attached to her mother through tightly clasped hands said something completely incomprehensible. Or so Emily thought, until the mother responded with an enthusiastic "I know!"

At which point Emily was certain they were commenting on the absurdity of the prosecutor showing such age standing, well, where she was standing. Maybe thinking she was contemplating a purchase for her daughter?

How embarrassing.

Her daughter. If she was—she wasn't—but if she was…would it be a girl?

She wasn't.

Should she buy the white box with pink lettering? The purple with white letters? Or the blue? Hands at her sides, she wasn't ready to touch any of them. To be seen touching them.

Dear God, she was going to have to walk up to the register and pay for it.

Bad idea, visiting a drugstore so close to her office. To the courthouse. Any judge she appeared before, any attorney she argued against, could walk in. See her.

Gulping, she glanced around to make certain she had the aisle to herself. What if someone in her own office saw her?

Turning, she stepped quickly into the next aisle. Took some deep breaths to calm down. Focused on potato chips and other bagged snacks. But couldn't contemplate buying any. Not until she knew for sure that she wasn't pregnant…

Just get the damned thing.

With anxiety threatening to tear through her, Emily

strode back around the corner, picked the first box her hand touched—purple with white lettering—and looked straight ahead as she took it to the register.

She had to know.

A practical woman would take care of the situation by finding out the facts. And she was the most practical woman she knew.

There was no line at the register. Speeding up before someone could round a corner and get ahead of her, she stared at a candy display as she put the box on the counter. She'd never seen the cashier before in her life. Within seconds the box and all the things it hinted at were encased inside a plastic Duane Reade pharmacy bag, covered by the chocolate bar she'd thrown on top of it and further buried within the satchel that served as her purse.

She had a challenging caseload awaiting her. Had to get the test behind her so she could give her career—which pretty much encompassed the entirety of her daily life—her complete focus.

And she had to do it without anyone, even the hot dog vendor on the corner, ever knowing that there was the slightest hint of a possibility that she could actually have a child growing inside her.

Frigid February air hit her as she pushed through the door, freezing her skin and her feelings, as, pulling her long black coat tighter with the belt at the waist, she barreled forward. Of course the light would turn green as soon as she hit the corner. Hunching a bit against the chill, she awaited her turn to cross, wanting to chuckle over the absurdity of her little errand.

Fear stifled every ounce of lightness from her soul. She couldn't be pregnant. Other than one ending-in-disaster engagement two decades before, she'd never even been in a serious relationship. The no-strings-attached liaison she'd had with Cormac Colton—a stupendous PI, gorgeous, but also so much younger than her that he'd still been filled with that vibrant belief that he could change the world—had not ended well.

One week with her and he'd abruptly said he was done. There'd been no conversation. No explanation. Or even a casual "see ya around." He'd been out.

Finished with her.

She could not be carrying his child. Shivering with cold, and dread, she saw traffic slowing. Stood up straight, ready to cross over to the courthouse, and lost all air as a thump against her back, around her shoulder, shoved her off balance and, propelled her to the opened door of a black SUV.

"What!" she hollered, shoving against the force trying to take over her body. The satchel hanging cross ways on her body didn't help her any, but she didn't let it slow her down. With a kick and a screamed demand to stop, she slapped out at her attacker, catching the side of his head with a whack. People surrounded them.

There'd be a pool of witnesses.

In spite of her blows, her abductor shoved her off

the curb and, with a hand on her head, was trying to force her down into the vehicle.

"No!" She screamed again, rearing back, bracing herself against the outside of the vehicle. The big gloved hand at her head pushed harder and her forehead hit the doorjamb just as she stomped on the man's foot.

And...

Then she was free. Her accoster was hauled off her, and half gasping, half sobbing, she stepped back up on the curb, feeling surrounded by a wall of gaping bystanders.

She heard the assailant utter "I'll get you next time" as he dove into the back seat of the SUV, which then sped off.

Among the crowd of onlookers she spotted dark hair and the back of wide coated shoulders. Dark hair that seemed professionally mussed. With a wayward spike of hair to the left of his collar. She saw the hardly noticeable little strand as the man turned.

No.

She was hallucinating.

Had lost her mind in the fray.

Gripped her bag to her side, still shaking, vaguely aware, in the mere seconds that had passed, that multiple voices were speaking to her.

She only heard the words from one.

"Emily, did he hurt you?"

She noted the concern. Stared.

"Call the police," the man hollered as he stood inches from Emily, his dark eyes filled with a concern that touched her far more deeply than her abductor had done.

"Already done," another male voice said.

"And an ambulance," her rescuer continued. For a man barely in his thirties, Cormac Colton had way more confidence and authority than she'd have expected.

Cormac. He was really there. Not just a figment of her way-too-harried state of mind. "I don't need an ambulance," she said then, finding her own stash of commanding tone, as the light changed again and she stepped off the curb to cross the street.

"Emily." He reached for her shoulder, not with force, but in an attempt to keep her there. "You need to talk to the police."

"Send them to my office. ADA Emily Hernandez," she announced to the crowd in general and, turning her back, hurried onto the crosswalk before the light could change. If the cops didn't show up, she could call them from there.

Arriving at the other side of the street, she stepped up onto the sidewalk, with Cormac right there beside her.

"I'm fine. You can go." She gave him as much of a dismissive tone as she could muster. Shaking harder.

Someone had just tried to kidnap her!

And the man who'd dumped her had suddenly shown up out of thin air to save her?

Her satchel...the box... Cormac Colton crowding her space... She hugged her bag with both hands. Held it close.

"I'm coming with you," the far-too-memorable voice said beside her. "I'll need to give my statement to the police as well."

As good as she was at coming up with logical arguments, she came up blank. Because of the bump to her head? She reached her hand up, but the skin was hardly tender enough to warrant a bruise.

The best sex she'd ever had was accompanying her to her office, where a pregnancy test would be sitting in her satchel and police officers would be waiting for her victim statement.

She'd almost been kidnapped! Who wanted her? And for what? She tried to focus on recent cases, threats made or perps she'd put away now getting released, but came up completely blank on all of it.

Cold and breathless, she wanted to cry.

And silently cursed her luck instead.

What in the hell had she done to deserve such cruel twists of fate?

Adrenaline pumping, Cormac strode next to the feisty prosecutor, keeping his body as close to her as he could without actually touching her again.

He was not allowed to touch her. Not unless it was a life-and-death situation. Her life.

His rule. Issued firmly to himself two months before when he'd broken off his liaison with her.

She didn't speak.

He focused on everything and everyone around them. Shielding her from behind, watching what was ahead. Even inside the courthouse and getting to her office. Didn't matter to him if either of them knew the people they passed. Until they figured out why someone had just tried to force her into a vehicle, everyone was suspect.

She made a beeline behind her desk, still clutching the satchel she wore, but didn't sit down. "You stalking me?" Her tone was challenging, not scared.

Colton's head turned, his gaze swinging toward the door he'd just come through, only to find that no one was there. Turning back, he saw her staring at him with an air of "how dare he" about her. "You're talking to me?" Shaking his head, he started to feel like he was in some kind of bizarre nightmare.

First, the near kidnapping, and now this?

Yeah, he'd been kind of dreading seeing her again—for a few reasons—but...

"Yes. How else do you explain turning up at the exact moment I'm the target of a kidnapping? If that's what it was. If you think this is some kind of joke..."

"Emily!" He raised his voice enough to get her attention. Figured shock was getting to her.

She blinked, didn't take her question back.

"Of course I'm not stalking you," he told her.

"You could be. With your stellar PI skills, how would I know?"

Mouth gaping, he stared. Was she serious?

"You seriously think I'd stalk you?" He couldn't even compute that one.

With a visibly deep breath, she sank to her chair, her satchel on her lap. She was still clutching it with both hands. "No, of course not."

She looked back up at him. "But you have to admit, it's odd that just when someone tries to accost me, you're suddenly right there…"

"What we need to be talking about is who's out to get you," he said then, coming closer, but only to sink into the chair across from her desk. One they'd stupidly, stupendously, had sex in. He had to sit so he didn't keep staring at the damned thing.

Where in the hell were the police? He grabbed his phone, intending to call one of his relatives to find out who was on duty in the area, but the look in her eyes stopped him.

A mixture of authority—and fear. Almost to the point of self-doubt. Emily was one of the most confident women he'd ever met. Which had been part of the incredible turn-on…

"I need to know why you were there," she said then.

Eager to help where he could, he sat forward, elbows on the arms of the chair. "I was on my way to see you," he told her. "To ask you about the case Humphrey Kelly was about to testify in when he went missing. You were the ADA…"

The seeming relief that flashed across her expression was confusing, too. Why else would he have been there? Had she really thought he'd been watching her? The idea was ludicrous. He was the one who'd broken off things between them.

Cut them off at the quick, was more like it.

To the point of rudeness.

And…she was grasping at straws. Trying to find

reason for the events that had just transpired. She had to be scared out of her wits. It was the only explanation that made sense out of her focusing more on his sudden appearance than on the kidnapping he'd thwarted.

You'd think she'd be grateful to him.

Thanking God he'd been there.

"I've already been asked about that case three times. He's a psychiatrist, was scheduled to give an expert witness testimony that we didn't really need to get a conviction and he didn't show up. That's all I know."

Humphrey was so much more. But he'd get to that. At the moment they had to figure out what had just happened, who wanted her, for what. Secure her safety until they found out.

He'd been about to tell her so when two uniformed officers he didn't know showed up at the door of her office.

And, glad to have them there, ready to work toward Emily's well-being, he put his own concern on the back burner while they did their job.

Chapter 2

The officers took thorough reports. Suggested that Emily not walk along the streets any more than was necessary while they looked into things, warning her to stay away from the curb, to try to walk in the middle of throngs rather than alone and close enough to buildings to duck inside if need be. But not close to alleys or doorways where someone could haul her inside.

Basically, they scared the heck out of her.

Their departure was a relief, more so because she expected Cormac Colton to go with them. She'd already given him the little she knew about Humphrey Kelly's disappearance. And his brother was a detective. He had a sister who was a cop. And other family who were members of the NYPD network. Knowing him, he'd figure out who'd been stupid enough to try to drag her off a busy street and into a car in the middle of the day.

So that was one good thing about the day.

About him.

Except that, as the officers left, even as Cormac took a few steps outside her door with them, he didn't actually go. Instead, after those couple of yards had enlarged the distance between him and her, he spun around and came back.

Filling her with cold and dread.

She couldn't help him. Even if she knew more about Humphrey than she realized, she'd have to deal with someone else. The detective on the case. Not the hired PI. She and Cormac Colton could absolutely not work together again.

She'd point-blank refuse if she had to.

If it came to that.

If he forced the issue.

"I'm fine now," she told him as he reentered the room. "You don't have to hang around."

"You were just…"

A wave of her hand, a strong shake of her head, cut him off. "Getting threatened is a job hazard," she blurted out. And then more words tumbled out on top of them. "I get threatening emails and phone calls, too. Mostly untraceable. I'm used to them."

She couldn't let him see her fear.

He'd once told her they were perfect for each other.

And now she needed him to get the hell out. She had to pee on a stick and prove to herself that she wasn't pregnant so she could quit acting like a complete ninny and get busy figuring out who'd tried to haul her off. To concentrate and remember a smell, a ring or scar, anything familiar. Because as the police had questioned her, she'd had nothing.

Except the faces of potential witnesses.

And the man who'd ultimately been in exactly the right place at the right time and saved her from God knew what…

He was standing there, watching her. Letting her ramble.

He'd risked his life for her.

"I didn't even thank you." Her tone softened. "You possibly just saved my life." Chills of horror, of fear—and of supreme gratitude—passed through her as she stared at him.

Then, when he shrugged and gave her that warm, "we've got a thing" look, she immediately broke eye contact with him. Fidgeted.

Inadvertently kicked the satchel she'd dropped to the floor at some point during their interviews with the police officers.

And remembered the purple box.

She felt no gratitude at all now toward the man who'd, two months before, contributed to one of her current scares. Potentially a life-altering one. How dare he sit there and smile kindly at her like their little fling was a fond memory and nothing more?

"Dare I hope I won enough good favor, maybe added to the fact that we know each other, to trade for a bit more detail on the case Humphrey Kelly was testifying on the day he disappeared? He was here at the courthouse. Disappeared right before he was due to testify. It just seems logical that there's some connection. Anything you can tell me, however inconsequential you might think it to be, might help."

"I have nothing else to give you," she told him, refusing to let Cormac see any chinks in her armor. "He was simply going to testify that the accused was of sound mind and body. That's it. The testimony was merely a formality. Just a statement for the record."

"Please, Emily." His gaze bore into her, as though he could, with just a look, compel her to give him whatever he wanted.

Because, for a short time, he'd been able to do just that? Because she'd wanted what they did as badly as he had…

"While I'm officially working the Kelly disappearance as part of the team my brother put together, this is far more than a case to us. Humphrey Kelly is like an uncle to me. He's not biologically related, but he pretty much raised me after my widowed father died when I was fourteen."

Her heart lurched. She hadn't known he'd been that young when his father died. Hadn't had time to ask, due to the amount of time they'd spent in bed together during the one week that their *thing* had lasted.

She couldn't let him suck her in again. Every second he was there agitated her more. "I've told you what I know." Sorry if she sounded harsh, but she needed him gone.

"There's got to be something more." Cormac didn't relent. Or seem to get the hint that he'd overstayed his welcome. "Was there some reason someone wanted the defendant to appear less than stable? Who'd have stood to gain from such a ruling?"

"The defendant is Evan Smith. He's on trial for shooting to death three people after a bar fight. That's all public knowledge, so you obviously already have it. Dr. Kelly's testimony was merely a formality, and that's all I know about his involvement. Dotting i's and crossing t's. You're the guy who has a passion for the truth." She shot the words at him as pressure built inside her. "How can you expect me to come up with facts I don't have?"

How could anyone expect her to confront the facts she did have without knowing the whole situation? What did it mean that Cormac Colton was standing in her office, having just probably saved her life, while she was sitting with her calf resting against the satchel that held the test that was going to give her the one fact she needed most at the moment?

Needed even more than knowing who'd just attempted to kidnap her.

Was she pregnant? Had her life changed on a dime without her knowledge? Or choice? She was forty-three years old! She couldn't be a new mom.

Had whoever was after her just threatened the life of her child, too?

Had karma brought Cormac to the rescue just in time?

To save his own child?

Panic rode over all sense of logic, leaving her in a haze of truths and questions and fear, while the man who'd upended her life stood there watching it all.

"You hate deception, Cormac," she said with anger coming forth as her defense, filling her voice with accusation. "Yet now you want me to come up with some magical piece of evidence that isn't there?"

Pulling back as though shocked, he opened his mouth, but she didn't give him a chance to speak—to confuse her more.

"Speaking of which," she fumed, "didn't you deceive me just a little when you led me to believe that our liaison was mutually beneficial in a long-term sense, since we'd discovered that we were both adamantly against anything more than great friends with benefits when schedules fell in line? And then just one week in, just a few weeks before Christmas, you abruptly cut me off, as though you'd suddenly discovered I was a murderer or something…treating me like little more than…" She stopped, midsentence. Hearing herself.

Horrified with herself.

All the problems she was facing that morning, and she was going to bring *that* up?

The man might be equally to blame for the cause of the stark panic that had driven her steps to the store that morning, but…he didn't know.

And…if she was…he'd have to know.

The thought choked all other words from her throat.

Cormac steeled his emotions as the most vibrant, sexy woman he'd ever known seemed to be falling apart in from of him.

Needing him, even if she didn't realize it.

As strong and capable as she absolutely was, she'd been abducted less than an hour before, would have been hauled away if he hadn't been able to intervene at the last second. But for a moment there, she'd lost all say over her life, as, in spite of her fighting back, her kidnapper had succeeded in taking control of her.

Cormac was being an ass, completely unlike himself, trying to make his search for Humphrey more important than the trauma she'd just suffered. His uncle's life was vital. But so was hers.

Nor was he going to be able to pretend seeing her again hadn't hit him. Hard. Try as he might. No way was he going to just be able to walk away again. Not until he knew she was out of danger.

"Things aren't always what they seem," he said, with the intensity simmering between them lacing his tone as well.

She'd accused him of being duplicitous in starting a long-term sexual relationship with her and then just cutting it off.

Truth stung.

But what would she have had him do? Tell her that he'd broken his own rules, her rules, too—*their* rules—by starting to fall for her as more than a no-strings-attached liaison? Like some kid panting over a real woman.

Which was probably what she'd have thought of him, faulting his youth to her eleven years more of experience for his inability to follow through on their agreement to keep things casual.

And even if she hadn't, it wouldn't have mattered. He was most definitely not losing himself to the vagaries of emotion that blinded him to the truth, that led to lost lives, a second time in his life. One dead lover was enough.

"I'm going to need a list of possible suspects," he said then, his tone brooking no refusal. He continued, "Threats you've received, anonymous and otherwise, anyone who might want to hurt you, all the cases you've worked on, no matter how far back, since someone you put away, someone bearing a grudge, might have recently been released from prison…"

He broke off as all expression left her face. He'd gone too far. Too fast. But…

"I don't need your help."

He could see how she'd feel that way. But he couldn't just walk out on her. All het up, fueled by adrenaline, and something more he couldn't name, he was a little brutal in his delivery of the truth. "You're in danger, Emily. Real danger. With no idea where it's coming from or when or how it'll be back. And finding dangerous guys who know how to get lost is what I do. You know I'm good at it." They'd met working a case together. "You seriously want me to just walk out of here and leave you with no answers? You want to have to walk in the middle of the sidewalk, finding crowds to get lost in, to be afraid of what might be just behind you or waiting in a doorway to get a second chance at you? I can see the fear emanating from you..."

With both hands on her desk, she stood, facing him, visibly trembling, and said, "You really want to know the greatest source of my fear, Cormac?"

"Absolutely." He'd go head-to-head with her on that one. No question at all.

She didn't argue with him even for a second, perplexing him with the ease of her capitulation, until he realized she was reaching for something. On the floor, by her feet.

Was she about to pull a gun on him and order him out?

He knew the thought was ludicrous. Had no merit, but he couldn't figure out...

She had a box in her hand. Cutesy purple with white lettering. He didn't get it.

Until...he did.

Then he didn't know what to do. Couldn't find a single coherent thought.

They were encapsulated by a swarm of unidentified life-threatening danger and she'd just dropped a pregnancy test on the desk between them.

"We used protection."

On the verge of flying off the handle, propelled by the myriad of emotions coursing through her, Emily took his words to be his way of asking if he was the father.

Ready to blast him for the insult—she wouldn't be sharing the news with him if he wasn't—she took one look at the whiteness around his lips, the blank look in his usually compelling dark eyes, and said, "I know. And listen, really, even if it failed, at my age, there's little chance that I'd actually get pregnant from one instance of escaped biological product. More likely, I'm going through the change of life early, getting sporadic with my cycle. I just started to wonder 'what if' to the point of interfering with my normal focus and had to make sure. If you hadn't been standing here trying to pressure me at a time when I'm already feeling about as much pressure as I can take, you wouldn't ever even have known…"

She watched him. And just kept babbling. Until his gaze homed in on her in that way he had of making her feel like she was the only thing he saw. Then her words stilled midstream.

"You're two months late?" It was like he was leaning over the desk instead of standing in front of it. Cupping her face with his hand rather than clutching the edge of her desk with white-knuckled fingers.

She nodded. There was no condemnation. Or anger.

"You ever been late before?"

Not a whole two months. Not even six weeks. She shook her head.

"Then let's go take the test."

"Cormac…"

"Seriously," he said, straightening, his arms folded against the muscled chest that still appeared in her dreams. Or in her mind's eye at inconvenient times during the day. "This is huge. For both of us. We need to know. Now. Let's do this."

If she hadn't been so het up, she might have smiled. Her decade-plus-younger lover was so vibrant, still believing that he could change huge portions of the world just by needing it so. That intensity had been part of what had drawn her to him—and, for a brief time, she'd felt that she was that young again. Or at least, had experienced reinstilled belief that her work, her life, made a real difference…

Licking her lips, she nodded toward the box on her desk. "The test… It's not an 'us' thing, Cormac. I do it alone."

With a shrug, he picked up the box. "I meant, let's get the results," he said as he handed it to her. "We need to know if an attempted kidnapping, on top of Humphrey's kidnapping—which could make it two people from the same case going missing, by the way—is all we're dealing with."

She took the box. There was no other logical choice.

And slipped into the small private half bath attached to her office, hoping she wasn't so bothered by him just outside the door that she developed a shy bladder and couldn't pee.

Chapter 3

Her bladder wasn't shy.

"You coming out?" Cormac called, so close to the door she imagined it vibrated with his energy.

Standing there holding the plastic handle, shaking now knowing that her future fate was imminent, she called back, "It takes three minutes to register results."

"Waiting is the part we can do together." She heard a brush against the door, like he was leaning against it. Or ready to join her inside the room.

He wouldn't. She knew him well enough to know that he'd respect a closed door. But the result she was waiting for was equally important to him.

Device in hand, held flat, she opened the door. He

wasn't noticing her at all. And was making her more nervous, when she hadn't imagined it was possible to be any more ready to explode. "Don't stare at it."

He glanced up at her, assessing her face, and she almost told him to go ahead and stare at the plastic test stick. But she stared back at him instead.

If she was pregnant…her child was his, too.

For the two weeks she'd been in denial and then working herself up, she'd been thinking in terms of her. Her life. Mammoth changes.

Cormac Colton had walked out. Made it clear he was done with her. She'd never made it to the part where he'd be affected, too, by the world-changing accident.

Not as much as her, of course. He could walk away. She couldn't.

"What's a plus mean?"

Her gaze shot to the apparatus in her hand the second she heard his words. The plus sign in the screen was unmistakable. Clear as day. Not even a little bit faint.

And then, as her hand shook uncontrollably, the weighty piece of plastic was taken away. Cormac set it on the desk.

"Positive. It means positive," he said, his tone far off and unfamiliar to her.

Positive.

She was pregnant. Sinking down to the chair in front of her desk, she stared at the piece of plastic on her desk. Roiling with emotion, she thought for a second there she was going to be sick, but something completely unexpected nestled within the madness swirling inside her. Surreal elation.

Yeah. There it was. Who'd have thought…

"I'm going to have a baby." And she wasn't completely devastated by the thought. In fact, the preparation she'd been busy doing—getting herself ready to know that she'd never ever have a child, even though she'd mentally taken the possibility off her table years before—slipped away unneeded.

Filled with an entirely new kind of energy, feeling like she didn't know herself at all, suffused with the same kind of single-minded determination that had built her successful career, she grabbed the stick. Thought about saving it. A memento.

"I can do this." She didn't know how. Stood through a wave of terror as she thought about buying baby stuff, and then, looking straight at Cormac, said, "I can do this."

Alone. Just as she always did pretty much everything. Made her decisions, bought her apartment, paid her bills, built her career, cooked her dinners, decorated and…and… She'd learn the rest.

She was a good learner. A quick learner.

Her parents, retired to Florida, would teach her how. They'd been great at it.

Her parents…

"You're pregnant." Cormac's tone wasn't quite questioning, but it had none of his usual notes of confidence. She stared up at him. He stood between the desk and the bathroom door with his fingers pulling at the collar of the pullover he'd had on under his coat.

"Yeah." She hadn't really comprehended the idea, either.

"We should get married. We're here, at the courthouse. We can file for a license now and appear before the judge tomorrow. My older brother, Sean, he's looking into things like that. He told me. Twenty-four hours is the wait time."

He didn't want to marry her. He'd dropped her like a hot potato. She was eleven years older than him. Had more wrinkles than he did.

He wasn't serious. Was in shock. Reacting. And her treacherous heart, leaping as it had, needed to get itself in check. A conversation she'd be having with it forthwith.

"I'll never marry a man who doesn't love me," she said. And then, hating the needy sound of that added, just as succinctly, "A man I don't love."

His nod was immediate. Confirming her belief that he hadn't meant the proposal.

Almost to the point of insulting.

"Let's sleep on the idea and reconvene on it later," he added several seconds too late.

"Sounds good. I'll call you tomorrow."

Right. That's what she was going to do. But she was glad to have the conversation over so quickly. And if a small, small, tiny, minute part of her was disappointed that he didn't seem even the least bit happy, she didn't give it enough attention to matter.

After all, she was old enough to know better.

He'd been dismissed.

Truthfully, one part of him wanted out of there probably more than she wanted him gone.

Stunned, he stood there with one clear goal. He could not leave her.

The woman had gotten under his skin a couple of months earlier in a way no other woman had, which was why he'd broken things off with her so abruptly. Because he absolutely would not ever again be in a relationship where emotion was the prime component keeping him there.

But she'd nearly been abducted.

And now she was carrying his kid? No way he could walk out on that.

"Sleeping on things, talking tomorrow, that's all good," he said, hating his seeming lack of control over anything in that moment. "But there's this morning's event…"

"I'll be fine," she interrupted.

"You were almost kidnapped," he continued, holding up his hand, "and before you tell me again that threats come with the job, I know damned well that abduction is not a part of your average business day. Beyond that, had you been taken, had your life been in danger, my kid's life would have been, too."

He gave her a chance to argue that, meeting her

gaze to gaze. Almost daring her to tell him he was wrong.

Her silence spurred more words from him, things he was making up as he went along. "I think that at least until the police, and I, have a chance to investigate this morning's incident, you should stay with me. It's not like you've never been to my place. You know there's space there for you…"

They'd had sex on the bed in his spare room.

"You know how easy it is for you to catch a cab to work from there, but we'll need to talk about you coming to the office at all, until this guy is caught…"

She wasn't immediately jumping down his throat. Which scared him.

And satisfied him at bit, too.

"You're a bit more vulnerable now that we know you're pregnant." He pushed home his advantage. "And as the father, I have a responsibility to the kid as well. You staying at my place allows me to take care of all sides of the situation to the best of my ability."

She might think her decade on him gave her wisdom he'd yet to gain, but he didn't buy that for a second.

He had no idea how it was going to work, her actually staying at his place rather than visiting for hot and heavy sexual encounters. No idea how he'd be with a woman in his private domain—most particularly her. Didn't even want to think about her naked in the shower, sleeping down the hall or even eating dinner at his table, for that matter. But he didn't take back the offer.

Wouldn't even consider doing so.

It spoke to his shocked state that it took him a bit to realize she wasn't saying no.

"No one would think to look for you there," he said softly. No one but the two of them had any knowledge of what had transpired between them. Not only had it been extremely short-lived, but they'd both gone out of their way to make sure that they weren't seen together.

They'd met working on a case. Neither of them had wanted anyone to think them less than professional or fully committed to their careers.

More than that, they'd made sure that no one had a chance to think that there was more to their association than would ever be there.

A shared kid kind of threw that all to hell.

And mattered not at all in the moment. He had to convince her to go home with him, to give him a chance to figure out who'd tried to kidnap her and to keep her—and the kid—safe in the meanwhile.

"Please, Emily." Begging wasn't beneath him apparently.

And worth every ego-killing second he stood there waiting. Then she finally nodded.

With her work her life, and her retired parents her only family, Emily stood in her office, trembling, realizing that other than people she was friendly with at work, she was completely alone in the city. With someone after her and a baby to protect.

Giving in to Cormac's request that she stay with him seemed the best choice. She wouldn't let her guard down, though. The man had been all enthusiasm and great talk one minute and then gone the next, but until she had a chance to assimilate the morning's events, to let the police—or Cormac if he really intended to help—find her accoster, she saw nothing wrong in allowing a father to protect his kid. The fact that the child resided inside her body made her presence with the two of them a basic necessity.

But…

"It has to be understood that the liaison that ended between us is still over," she said, reminding herself of the cutthroat way he'd walked out of her life. "There is absolutely nothing between us except the child."

Child sounded so much more distant in her head, less intimate. Hearing herself say the word aloud, not so much.

She couldn't believe she was going to be a mother.

A replay of the kidnapping flashed across her mind, and fear—new and much sharper—sliced through her. The baby… She might never have become a mother. Her little one might never have known life.

"You said something about wanting access to my cases, to people I've prosecuted who were recently released from prison and…other things," she said, as that near-abduction memory loomed, squeezing air out of her lungs anew. Turning, she spread her arm to sweep across her desk. "It's all yours. And, actually, I can access most of it from my laptop. It's secure. I go online through my phone, also secure, so I can work from home. Or...other...places."

On high speed suddenly, filled with panic-laced octane, she gathered up the few hard copy files she needed, her laptop, a legal pad and pen, which she shoved with the laptop into her satchel, and turned toward the door.

Cormac, to his credit, didn't say a word.

He just waited while she did what she had to do and then followed her out.

Cormac took his cues from Emily, giving her all the space he could, until she announced that she'd need to stop by her place on the way to his. No way he could let that happen.

"We have to assume that whoever is out to get you knows where you live," he pointed out, in spite of the fact that he knew he was likely scaring her.

She needed to be afraid. In her situation, a good dose of fear would go a long way toward keeping her safe.

But he wasn't totally without empathy. "I'm calling a cab to pick us up outside the judge's secure entrance," he told her as he ushered her down the less used stairs rather than heading toward the elevator she'd intended to use. "Make a list of whatever you need and where to find it and I'll send my sister, Eva, to pick it up. She's always up for any favor I ask, and I am for her, too. She's in uniform, a noob, but fearless, in case anyone's lying in wait. And if someone is watching your place, he knows the police are watching it, too, watching for him."

"You never said you were close with your sister."

There were a lot of things he hadn't told her. Some genetic… He paled. "I also never told you I'm a twin." He dropped the information as lightly as he could. "Not identical, though, so I don't think that's a thing."

Two sacs, not one, so hopefully not genetic. But it wasn't like he really knew beans, one way or the other.

She'd stopped on the stairs, one up from him, mouth open, staring. Hard to believe that fit, lusciously curvaceous body with the dark wavy hair tumbling around it, that the determined woman who so confidently owned it, was pregnant with his baby.

"You're a twin."

"Yeah, but like I said, not identical."

"Brother or sister?"

"Brother. His name's Liam."

"Is he local?" With her standing up there looking down on him, he felt compelled to answer.

"Yeah. We're all working the Humphrey Kelly case together. My brother Sean, the detective—" he'd told her about Sean during the case work that had brought Cormac and Emily together in the first place "—Eva, Liam and I."

"Liam's a cop, too?"

"No, he's a stupidly rich dude who runs an awareness program for the precinct." He was also an ex-con, but that was a story for another, less stressful, probably-never-going-to-happen day. Unless she needed to know due to the kid.

He turned to head down the steps and heard her voice behind him.

"We were together seven nights in a row and you never thought to tell me you're a twin?"

She hadn't budged. So maybe the genetic thing was an issue still. Or she was just freaking out because it was a freaking out kind of day.

"I didn't tell you I had a sister who was a rookie cop, either."

"Yes, you did. The night you saw a missed call from her and then when you called her back, she didn't pick up."

Yeah. Eva had been on duty. He'd panicked for a second. Until Eva had texted that she'd get with him later. He'd forgotten about it the moment Emily's lips had touched his.

"You weren't used to her being on the streets yet," the assistant ADA reminded him as they continued down the stairs.

And he was reminded of just how good she was at remembering every detail about everything—and drawing concrete conclusions from the mix. It made her great at her job.

It had also made her a compelling and unforgettable companion. Emily Hernandez, unlike most women he'd spent time with, stimulated him, captivated him as much mentally as she did physically. Which was why he'd had to run, not walk, out of her door and not look back.

And while he was going to keep her firmly in his sights until he knew she was safe, he still wasn't looking back. With a baby on the way, him keeping his heart free from the kind of emotional entanglement that blinded him was now more critical than ever.

Chapter 4

Eva Colton wasn't the one who brought Emily's things. Emily had been curious to meet the young woman who'd followed her brothers into law enforcement.

Instead, as she stood in the spacious living area of Cormac's apartment, clutching the satchel hanging from her shoulder, trying to pretend she hadn't had sex on the couch just feet away from her, she watched him open his door to a Colton she did know, Cormac's older brother, Sean.

"Detective Colton," she said, stepping forward, reaching out her hand for a shake, needing to assert control over the situation before she lost hope of gaining any. That was before she realized he wasn't just there to see Cormac on business.

She didn't notice the duffle he'd had slung on his back until it slid forward as he reached for her hand. Instead of giving her a brusque shake, he slid the strap of the gym bag–looking carryall down his arm and handed it to her. "Eva asked that I give this to you."

So much for being the professional in control. Now they all knew she was staying with their brother. How embarrassing.

And…how to explain…

"Cormac told me that he gave you little choice but to use his guestroom until we get some things sorted out," Sean continued, seemingly having no trouble commandeering all of the control she'd been hoping to obtain. "I apologize for my brother's heavy-handedness in this matter and want you to know that if you'd rather be in a hotel or someplace else, we can assign an officer to keep you company. At least until we get an initial look at things…"

"I told Sean that I, um, insisted that you stay here, so that I can provide you with protection and also work with you to figure out who's after you. Since, you know, your abduction follows so closely behind Humphrey going missing, both events in or near the courthouse, and with both of you associated with the same case…"

He hadn't told his brother she was pregnant with his child, Emily translated the slightly awkward, completely unlike Cormac explanation.

She nodded. Looked Sean Colton in the eye, and said, "I'd just as soon stay here, if you don't mind," she told him. "I don't go anywhere I don't choose to go. I want this settled as soon as possible and intend to be as involved as possible in figuring out what happened this morning and why." Then she added, "In case Cormac didn't tell you, I'm paying your brother for his protection. I worked with him on a case a couple of months back and have hired him to work for me on this matter."

Cormac's gaze shot to her. She read the argument there, but didn't think he'd call her out in front of his brother. And she didn't budge from her stance. She'd come up with the idea of having Cormac officially work her case during the drive over from the courthouse. To keep things clean and tidy between them. She just hadn't mentioned her plan to him. But now it was official.

He'd argue when they were alone. And she'd offer to leave. She held the trump card in that particular matter.

And needed not to feel as though her pregnancy made her dependent on him.

"He didn't mention the money, no," Sean said, sliding a glance toward Cormac, who took her bag and headed toward the hall leading back to the bedrooms.

"We hadn't decided on terms when I spoke to you," Cormac said over his shoulder.

The way he'd taken her bag, brooking no argument, she knew she'd pissed him off, making him look bad in front of his brother. And, she acknowledged silently, that she probably could have found a better way to handle the situation.

"I'm here to let you know that I'm the detective who's been assigned to your attempted abduction case," Sean said, moving toward the far end of the room, just off the kitchen, to take a seat at Cormac's six-chair dining table.

Oh. "Does Cormac know?" she asked, as the father of her child came back out to join them.

"I did know, yes," he said then, his tone challenging as he looked at her. "Sean texted to say he was on his way over."

Okay, fine. Neither one of them was doing so well in the trusting-each-other-with-communication department. A complete antithesis to their dealings in the past.

She flashed Cormac a glance, nodded and looked at Sean with equal gratitude and acceptance as she pulled her laptop out of her satchel and said, "I can send each of you a list of my current cases right now. It'll take a little bit of time to research recent prison releases to gather up previous cases that would be more likely to have been involved, but I'll get on that right away."

Both men nodded, and Sean said, "I wanted to let both of you know that we got a license plate number on the SUV from witness statements and have already talked to the driver. He's employed by a private car service and was dispatched to a corner just a block from the courthouse to pick up a Tom Jones. That name mean anything to you?"

A slice of fear shot through her as Sean Colton's intent gaze focused on her. The near kidnapping… it had been real. Attached to a man with a name.

Frantically searching her memory banks, she shook her head slowly. Then turned back to her computer, and with fingers fumbling on the keyboard, ran a quick document search.

"I come up with Jones. And with Tom. But not together," she told both men.

"It's likely not the guy's real name," Cormac told her, his tone more empathetic than anything. Soothing her in the way he'd had from the first day she'd met him.

Emily wasn't, and never had been, a woman who needed soothing.

Finding her gaze holding on to the man for too long, she quickly glanced back at her screen and then over to Cormac's brother. If Sean noticed anything passing between the two of them, he was professional enough not to acknowledge it. Instead, he said, "Jones told the driver that his sister had gone off her meds, that she was out of her head and a friend of hers had called him and told him that she was headed to the courthouse to insist on seeing the judge who'd ordered her remanded to a mental health facility. He warned the driver that there was a possibility she'd risk being picked up."

"Where was the driver supposed to take them?"

Sean named a professional building not far from the courthouse. "Jones said that his sister's psychiatrist had offices in the building. We've got a basic sketch of the guy, but not much from surveillance footage so far. With the winter coat, it's hard to tell his build, and the hood he was wearing along with the scarf concealed his features."

She'd never even seen the man's face. Only the black leather of his coat on the arm around her, black gloves and shoes.

"Officers are going around the building now with a description and the sketch," Sean continued.

"And when the pickup went askew?" she asked, shuddering in spite of her attempt not to do so.

"The driver said Jones apologized, asked to be dropped off around the corner, paid cash and bugged out. The driver had the impression that the guy was frantic for his sister's safety because as soon as he paid, he ran off in the direction of the courthouse. The driver also called the police. We have a record of his 9-1-1 call coming in just after it all happened."

"What about surveillance tape from the pickup or drop-off sites?" Cormac's question was succinct.

"We haven't been able to locate any. Officers are still canvassing."

The brothers exchanged a serious glance, and Emily knew any hope she had that everyone would just blow off her little incident as a fluke—so that she could try to convince herself that's all it was— had died a painful death.

Until they found her would-be abductor, she was in real danger.

From him. And from her forced proximity to Cormac Colton, too.

The intensity of feelings the private investigator raised in her should be criminal.

The two cases Sean was most interested in, as far as Emily's involvement was concerned, were the two he was also most familiar with—the one involving Humphrey Kelly's testimony and the Lana Brinkley murder that Sean had had to turn over to investigate the Kelly disappearance.

The case involving Kelly's testimony had been put on hold due to the psychiatrist's absence, just until another expert could be called in to take Kelly's place. Getting Emily out of the picture wouldn't make any difference to that or in any way prevent the district from continuing on with the trial . With her gone, another ADA would simply be assigned to take over for her.

Same with the Brinkley murder in terms of its trial, but if Emily was onto something there that their prime suspect, Wall Street mogul Wes Westmore, didn't want getting out, he could have hired someone to get to Emily. To intimidate her into silencing some evidence he might suspect she has.

"I can't imagine what it would be," Emily told Sean as Cormac reached for the file cabinet in the closet behind his table, spun the dial to unlock it and pulled out his Westmore file.

He liked things spread out in front of him, where he could take them in all at once, a big picture, rather than flipping back and forth between screens.

"You all have more on the case than I do," she

said, opening her own Westmore file. "But I'm still going through it all, so there might be something here I'm going to pick up on. I'll jump in again as soon as we're done here."

A fist tightening in Cormac's gut had him biting his tongue rather than suggesting that Emily take a day or two off from work. At least until he'd had time to get a handle on things—both the kidnapping attempt and the baby she was carrying.

She wouldn't listen to him.

And truth was, he wasn't sure she should. As long as she worked from his place, she'd be reasonably safe. He didn't have a say in the rest of her choices.

Except…she did plan to have the baby, didn't she?

Did she even know?

He had a say in that.

And in what would happen to the child after it was born.

If she didn't want it, he'd take it.

And if she did…he'd insist on doing his part.

Thoughts flew through his mind as Emily let Sean know that she wasn't thrilled that he was off the Brinkley case. And with a blink, Cormac wondered how he could know, in the space of an hour or two, that he was ready to commit himself to being a father.

Well, not ready, at all, but committed to getting that way. He'd lost his dad young. Knew what it was like to get through high school without one. He wasn't doing that to his own kid.

"No offense, but I think Mitch Mallard is a blowhard," Emily was telling Sean, talking to Cormac's older brother as though they were familiar associates.

He supposed they could be. Just…when she and Cormac had been together, she'd never mentioned his brother.

But then neither had he. Quite purposely.

Family didn't play into what they had going on.

Family was the antithesis to it.

And they'd made a kid from that?

He'd long ago lost any fondness he had for fate. But this…twist of circumstance… Well, it…blew.

But… "We share your opinion of Mitch." Cormac jumped back into the conversation—to put an abrupt end to his own internal wanderings, but also to tell her what his brother technically could not.

"With the body nabbing happening so close to the courthouse, we have to consider that the perp could be someone within the courthouse," he said. Then, something that had occurred to him on the ride home. "Someone who knows your schedule." He spoke to his new houseguest, but looked to his brother as well.

Saw Sean nodding before the detective asked, "Can you think of anyone there that might have it in for you for some reason? Not necessarily work related."

The way Emily's brow furrowed when she was looking for answers had been one of the first things that had attracted his attention the first time he'd worked with her. The shape of her brows accented those big dark eyes, which were pools he could drown in.

And he nearly had the first time he'd jumped in. He'd come close to throwing away everything that mattered most to him, to forgetting all the painful lessons he'd learned. Had barely been able to get himself out.

No way he could go back in…

"Not that I can… I mean, there's this guy in the DA's office. He's young, egotistic, a good mind, but needs to slow down and think before he speaks if he hopes to make it… Anyway, he made a big deal about discovering some evidence that turned a case into something else entirely, one of my cases, and tried to go over my head to get his day in the sun, but it turned out that he almost blew my case and I called him on it. In front of people."

"What's this guy's name?" Cormac asked.

"Jason Willoughby."

"I'll look into him," Cormac told them both.

"You think it could be him? That this was just payback for embarrassing him?"

"If it was, don't for one second think that it means you're in less danger," Sean interjected. "Someone who'd go to those lengths to get back at a colleague… There's no telling what else he might do."

The stark expression that flitted across Emily's face made Cormac want to shut his brother up, even as he knew he'd have given her the same warning if Sean hadn't spoken first.

"The incident did have a personal feel about it," he said then.

"He wasn't just dragging me into the car—he was

holding me up against him," Emily added slowly, looking between the two of them. "I didn't even think about that until now."

Sean nodded, then offered, "Could be the only way he could get you into the car."

"Yeah, but the way he told her he'd get her next time… I heard his words," Cormac said. "It sounded like he had it in for her. Like he was making a promise specifically to her, not just to an ADA on a case. I heard real hate in his voice. We'll make a list of all possibilities from cases, but I want to pursue this personal angle, too," he told his brother.

Sean nodded, as Cormac had known he would. His brother might have age and experience on him, but he knew that Sean also respected his judgment implicitly. That the detective respected and relied on him.

As did a whole lot of other people. Including himself.

Which was precisely why he would never again lose his mind to the vagaries of being in love, or even get caught up in a long-term one-on-one partnership.

The reminder couldn't have come at a better time.

Standing, Sean nodded at Cormac and then, to Emily, said, "Keep me posted on whatever you come up with on the Westmore case," he said. "And if you think of anything, no matter how small, on the Kelly case…"

Emily nodded. "I will." Her tone was different when she spoke to Sean. More distant.

Somehow Cormac had to get her to talk to him like that, too.

"And listen to this guy," Sean said then, punching Cormac lightly on the shoulder. "He might be a pain in the ass, but he's the best there is at what he does. If anyone can find your answers and also get you through this unscathed, it's him."

It had been a while since Cormac had had the urge to deck his big brother. But that urge came knocking, hard, as he stood and, avoiding even a glance at Emily, practically pushed Sean toward the door.

He was no kid to be teased by his big brother—huge compliment included or not.

He might be eleven years younger than his recent lover, but when it came to the situations they were now facing, both the risk to her life and the kid she was carrying, they were complete equals.

Get 4 FREE REWARDS!

We'll send you 2 FREE Books plus 2 FREE Mystery Gifts.

FREE Value Over **$20**

Both the **Harlequin Intrigue®** and **Harlequin® Romantic Suspense** series feature compelling romance novels filled with heart-racing action-packed romance that will keep you on the edge of your seat.

HARLEQUIN
PLUS

Announcing a **BRAND-NEW** multimedia subscription service for romance fans like you!

Read, Watch and Play.

Experience the easiest way to get the romance content you crave.

Start your **FREE 7 DAY TRIAL** at www.harlequinplus.com/freetrial.